MAGGIE AND THE MAGIC TROUT

a novel by

Nate Greig

First published by Dog Ear Publishing
4011 Vincennes Rd
Indianapolis, IN 46268
www.dogearpublishing.net

dog ear
PUBLISHING

ISBN: 978-1-4575-5851-1

This book is printed on acid-free paper.

This book is a work of fiction. Places, events, and situations in this book are purely fictional and any resemblance to actual persons, living or dead, is coincidental.

Printed in the United States of America

Dedicated to my wife, mother and sister

Foreword

Go to the mountains I say. To the verdant valleys in between. Where the blue mist hangs above morning dew. Where the night sky shines a starlit hue.

Here an ancient beast may keep a home. Live upon this land, and freely roam.

Listen to your wild heart, free it from its fashioned cage. Feed your soul anew. And join me in a timeless age.

These pursuits of greatest worth. Dare I say invite rebirth.

Let the children play. Go to the mountains I say.

Feel the river sway. Go to the mountains I say.

CHAPTER

1

$\mathcal{A}$ small cloud of dust swirled up into the stale air of an open beam, A-framed attic. A hatched door had just been opened for the first time in long time. A young girl clopped up an old wooden ladder and clambered onto the attic floor, its splintered boards creaked beneath her petite weight.

Maggie looked around the dimly lit space in silence. Evening light filtered into the attic through a slitted vent from the other side of the room. Particles of dust flashed brightly as they drifted slowly in and out of the angled beams of light. Maggie watched them for a moment and felt compelled to cough. She shook the urge, raised her hand to the ceiling and flipped on the only light switch in the space. A dim incandescent bulb slowly cast the attic in soft yellow light.

Beat up cardboard boxes, old heavy trunks, antique furniture, large, black and white portraits of somber people dressed in old fashioned clothing, and milk crates filled with vinyl records were staged in no particular order around the crawl space. Maggie surveyed the room with intent. She shuffled over to the nearest stack of boxes looking at their labels, scribbled with black permanent marker. She was searching for one box in particular.

It was medium sized and well worn. The lid had been discolored from what looked to be a coffee spill as the stain was very dark and distinct. A perfect circle of the original color remained in the middle of the stain, likely protected by the very mug that had threatened to soil the box's contents. The box was labeled *"yearbooks"*. Maggie's father had taken it down the year before when he was preparing for a yard sale. Maggie had taken notice of it and asked about its contents. He replied with a quick, "It's nothing Sweetie" and swiftly stowed the box back into the attic.

Tomorrow was the last day of the school year for Maggie. She was a fierce and focused student. Much of her school year had been spent studying or playing sports. She would graduate from middle school with flying colors and enjoy one of her last summers of freedom before having to prepare for college and profession, and all of the responsibility and commitment that comes from those arenas. She had just received her first yearbook earlier in the day and doing so ignited her curiosity. She was immediately reminded of the abandoned box her father had uncovered. Maggie now wanted to explore the contents of that box. She quickly read the labels of all that had been stowed in the attic.

It was perched on top of an old nightstand alongside a stack of dust covered, framed photos. Maggie quickly hoisted the box down to the floor and opened up its coffee stained top. A row of cumbersome, hardcover books were organized upright with their spine, and title, filling the box neatly. Maggie considered which book to look for.

"Let's see," she thought "I know Dad was older. He would have graduated first. So Mom's would have been the most recent ones." Maggie grabbed the most recent book and searched for her mother. "She was probably a senior," surmised Maggie as she flipped through the crisp, glossy pages in search of class portraits. "What was her last name?" she tried to recall "Sarah... but what was her last name?" giving her memory a decent chance to recall, but instead ended up searching for any "Sarah" in the graduating class. Maggie found her in the the section with last names starting with "D".

"Douglas," she said contently "Sarah Douglas." Maggie's stomach knotted with excitement as she inspected her mother's features closely. She could see that they shared the same quaint, bulbous nose, and warm, broad smile, and sincere gaze, but her mother's hair was longer and straight, and naturally hung like a fine satin curtain. Maggie's was short and wavy and knotted easily as it grew past her shoulders.

It had been a long time since Maggie had seen a photo of her. As far as she knew, there were no other pictures of her in the house. The only time she was lucky enough to get a glimpse of her mother was while looking through family photo albums while visiting relatives during the holidays. She had learned early on not to ask questions about Mom as she was always received with hesitant, uncomfortable uncertainty. Maggie had no actual memory of her mother so she adapted relatively easily to living with the void. But holding Sarah Douglas' yearbook suddenly made her mother feel very much alive. For the first time, Maggie yearned to know about her mother.

"Maggie it's time to come down," boomed a familiar voice from below, "big day tomorrow," the voice said assertively.

Maggie closed the heavy book with a "thump" as though she had been caught reading something that she was not supposed to. She let out a deep sigh as she held the time capsule in her hands. "Okay dad!" she hollered back, trying not to sound frustrated. She tried to set the book back in its original space but something inside the gap between the other yearbooks blocked it from going all the way in. Maggie reached her hand inside the gap to move the obstruction. It was a book, a much smaller paperback. Maggie furrowed her brow in confusion. "I didn't see any paperbacks in there," she thought. Maggie picked up the small book and inspected it with great intrigue.

It was a very old book and well worn. The cover page had a soft ridge of exposed white running down its length where it had been accidentally folded in half and compressed in that state for far too long. The corners had been rounded and frayed from being taken on too many ventures in unsecured positions. The pages had stained yellow like the moustache of a chain smoker. As Maggie drew the article closer for inspection, a pasty aroma of age mixed with spice flurried into her nostrils. Maggie read the title, *"A Special Land"* written by *Johnny Muur*. She had never seen nor heard of the book. "It's odd that I didn't see it in there when I was looking around in the box." she pondered "I would have seen it. And why is *this* in with the yearbooks? Every other book in here is a yearbook." Maggie stared at the book inquisitively as she held it in her hands. After a moment she remember her father's instructions. She clutched the book to her chest, turned off the light and swiftly descended down the squeaky ladder to prepare for bed.

Later that night, as Maggie lay in her bed, she stared at the item of intrigue that had mysteriously crept into the yearbook box. It rested on her dresser on the other side of her small room. Its worn pages fanned away from each other giving the impression that it might pop open at any moment and spring to life. Maggie fell asleep with thoughts running through her mind. Thoughts of her mother, some writer named Johnny Muur, and his, apparently, "special land".

~

The first thing Maggie said when she heard the news was, "No way! I'm not going Dad." she stared at her father firmly from across the dining table.

Father looked at her from above his reading glasses and set down the newspaper he'd been perusing. He gazed at her for a moment and thought to himself, "She is growing up more and more with each passing day. She is such a strong girl, so independent, and smart. Just like her mother. It's only a matter of time before she'll be too busy for me."

"Now Maggie," he said, "I know that you have a very busy summer planned, and lots of cool things to do, but I want to show you a very special place. A place that my parents took me to when I was your age. We are going there in one week and that is final."

Maggie sighed, let her shoulders drop, and went back to eating her soggy cereal. Far from convinced, she recalled, "This isn't going to be like the time we visited Great Aunt Mimi. Is it? I had to spend the entire day help-ing her sew big, polka dotted underwear. The whole time that stinky, furry dog of hers kept drooling on me. And then she tried to pour me a glass of her dill pickle tea, gross!"

Father chuckled from behind his newspaper, "Now Maggie, I promise. This will be nothing like going to Great Aunt Mimi's." He looked at his watch, "Time to go to your last day of the school year. Let's not be late."

Maggie raised her eyebrows in surprise, took a large and hurried scoop of cereal. Amidst the chewing she said, "Okay Dad, but we will continue this discussion when I get back from school okay?"

Father smiled, "Okay sweetheart."

Maggie stared at the lifeless meal below her pensively. She sighed and looked back at him with intrigue "Where'd you say we're going again?" she asked.

Father bit the side of his lip and paused, not realizing he was holding his breath. At last he inhaled shallowly and let out an awkward breath. "Yel-lowsemite…" he said with hesitation in his voice, as if he had admitted to something that made him feel uncomfortable. "You're going to love it," he forced, almost coughing out the phrase.

Maggie eyed her father with a mixture of love and speculation. She had her doubts, and wanted to voice them, but decided it best to hide them for the time being and respond with a simple, "Let's go." She could see he was uncomfortable, but she could not explain the cause of it. "Was I being too bossy again?" she wondered. Either way, Maggie had too much respect for the man to question his judgment any further. From her ear-liest memories, Father had built himself to be a steadfast source of guid-ance and instruction, and though her curiosity and skepticism were well alit, Maggie knew it was only appropriate to go along amicably with his plan. Besides, he had never lead her astray before.

The last day of school passed by like a whitewater rafting trip through a swift and narrow canyon. Maggie did her best to avoid the chaos. A compromise of hysteria, glee and reflection graced the faces of Maggie's fellow classmates as they drifted by, laughing and screaming over their accomplishments. Maggie was present for the frivolity, but her attitude was more subdued. The recent events at home kept her thoughts occupied with the past and the future, and not so much with the present.

When it was all said and done, after the buses had collected all of their happy travelers, and all of the parents had picked up their giggling graduates, the school campus returned to its routine, peaceful quiet. Maggie then decided it was time to walk home. Her house was close. Two blocks down the street in an older neighborhood guarded by stately elm trees lining both sidewalks. She loved walking home. It was always placid. The tree's large green leaves shaded so well that it never got too uncomfortable to walk beneath them, even on those hot summer afternoons. Maggie loved listening to the drowning hum of cicadas in the trees above her. This was when she liked to think about all the things going on in her life. And this day was no different. She thought about the conversation she had earlier with her father, about going somewhere with him. "What did he call it again? Yellowsemite. What kind of name is that?" she wondered. "That doesn't sound special. That sounds confusing."

"I really don't think going there is in my best interest," she thought. "What could possibly be so important that we have to drive for days across the country just to go to a park? We'll probably be crammed inside the car. And my legs will cramp from having to sit forever. And what if I have to use the bathroom? I am NOT going at a rest stop!"

"Yep," she said aloud. "I should not be going. But I am." she frowned in dismay. But Maggie was very smart, and independent. "Well," she thought, "I might as well prepare myself. When I get home I'm going to learn as much as I can about where we are going and come up with a plan of action so that we don't get stuck in one of those catastrophes again. I'll make sure we have fun on this trip!" Maggie smiled proudly as the drone of the humming cicadas broke her concentration. She turned her head to the left to realize that she was in front of her house. She went to the mailbox, grabbed its contents and skipped excitedly into the house.

That night, after dinner, Maggie decided to get started. "Dad?" she asked.

"Yes Maggie?" replied Father.

"I need to use the internet to do some research," said Maggie.

Father looked up from washing the dishes. A thick mound of oily bubbles protruded above the dark granite countertop. Hot steam swirled thickly above the bubbles. With a look of perplexity he responded, "Of course Sweetie, but why do you need to do research now? Didn't you just finish your school year? Don't you want to talk to your friends on the phone or watch movies or camp in the backyard or something?"

Maggie continued to clear the table. She never turned back towards him. She was focused on the task at hand. "Yes Dad, I do, but those things will have to wait. Right now I really have to do some research. I'm not about to let you take me to this park of yours without having some backup options in case things don't go according to plan."

Father let out a loud laugh, "Now why would you think something like that?"

"I don't know Dad. Something unexpected always seems to happen whenever we get out of the house," answered Maggie absently as she wiped down the dining table with broad, arching strokes.

"Well if you say so my dear, but isn't that why we get out of the house in the first place?" he retorted.

Maggie paused and thought to consider what he had pointed out. She had never thought about it like that before. After a moment, she shrugged and said, "If you say so Dad," and walked away to learn about Yellowsemite National Park (or whatever it's called).

CHAPTER

2

For most, having to research can be a very boring affair. It is generally only done when one is forced to do so. This was not the case for Maggie, she loved to research, and she was really good at it. It was one of the many reasons why she was so smart. Maggie had a trick that made researching fun. She only researched things she was interested in. Fortunately for Maggie, she was interested in almost everything, so she liked to research pretty much anything.

Maggie flopped onto her comfortable mattress and wedged a large pillow at the bottom of her spine as she propped up against the headboard. She wiggled into comfort and grabbed her laptop. As soon as the search engine appeared she typed "Yellowsemite". Without delay a million matches presented themselves. She clicked on the first one at the top and began reading.

Yellowsemite or Grand Smoky Yellowsemite National Park is the nation's oldest and largest park. It has three major mountain ranges (Yellow, Semite, and Smoky) as well as several smaller ranges. It has many lakes, the largest being Yellowsemite Lake, and also possesses large valleys and plains that host large herds of herbivores that have gone extinct elsewhere. Yellowsemite Valley rests on top of an active volcanic area which, in turn, produces active geysers, vents, thermal pools, fumaroles, and lava fields. First inhabited by the Ahwanchee tribe, Yellowsemite was designated a National Park after being rediscovered by Johnny Muur. Without his efforts we would likely not have this iconic national treasure.

Maggie shot up from the screen in surprise. For a moment she stared ahead with a blank stare and open mouth. She took a quick shallow breath and slowly drew her gaze to the new found book that laid upon her dresser. She kept her eyes on the book and hesitantly slid the computer from her lap, squirmed off of the bed, and tiptoed to it. She held it in her hands and looked the cover over in wonder. "A Special Land," she whispered, "by Johnny Muur."

As Maggie read the title, the hairs on the back of her neck stood up. "Okay" she voiced, "it's just a book, it's just a book". She tried to rationalize the situation but her thoughts ran wild, "I don't get it. The only book mixed in with the yearbooks is this thing? That's insane. What does this mean? Am I supposed to read it? Am I in danger? Is this a sign?" Maggie closed her eyes tightly as she sought a resolution. "Think, think," she said aloud, "what does Dad say?" Maggie closed her eyes tightly and inhaled as if trying to calm her wild thoughts. At last, his words of wisdom came to her, "Trust your feelings". Maggie smiled a little, recalling the many instances when Maggie had struggled with making a decision. Her father's simple words had never let her down. She blew out a breath of air and relaxed her shoulders.

"Trust your feelings," she said confidently. Maggie held the book up in front of her. She had regained her composure. "I'm going to read you," she said with a grin. "but not quite yet. I'll wait 'til we get on the road". Maggie set the book down on the dresser. She walked back to her bed buoyantly, a look of underlying confidence and excitement flushed across her face. She rested back into comfort against the headboard and continued researching with her laptop. The next portion of the webpage read *"park origin"*. She clicked on the link and began reading.

> *A long time ago, when people were still exploring the wild places of the country, there weren't any rules about using the land that was being explored. People could go pretty much anywhere, and do pretty much anything.*

"That's cool!" thought Maggie.

This may sound cool and sometimes it was, but sometimes it wasn't cool. Back then, everything was plentiful, and there weren't many people. So when people used the land, it didn't seem like much harm was ever being done. But as more people came around, there was less, resources, usable land and open space. And that's when problems started to arise. The massive, ancient forests of the east were quickly chopped down for building houses. The savannahs of the south were all tilled over for vast farmland. The beautiful rivers of the west became large reservoirs to store water for the cities and farms below, and later to make electricity.

"So what?" thought Maggie. "Houses are good, we need farms and cities, and everybody needs water and electricity." She read on:

We needed these resources from nature in the past, and we need these resources now. The only problem was that our country was becoming very bland and boring. Everywhere that people went, it was one city after another, one farm after another, one reservoir after another. The country looked the same wherever one traveled, quite boring. And the people living there became boring because of this. It all looked the same, so everyone acted the same. It wasn't very long before the people realized they had a serious problem on their hands. 'We are totally boring!' they said. 'What has happened? I wasn't this boring when I was a kid.' Everyone was worried. They didn't want to be boring so they called a huge meeting to solve their boring problem. After many hours, they came up with a solution. The Boring Police!

The Boring Police, or "BoPo" for short, were police officers who made sure that no one ever acted boring. They would walk through the cities and the farms, and swim across the reservoirs, to stop people from being boring.

"OMG!" thought Maggie, "This is so ridiculous. How can this idea possibly work?" She read on:

This idea was ridiculous and the BoPo never stopped anyone from being boring. In fact, people became even more boring because they all stayed inside their house, afraid to go out, because they couldn't afford to pay any more tickets for being boring. The BoPo had become so accustomed to ticketing people, that they started handing out tickets to anyone they came across.

Except for one man, Johnny Muur. Johnny was an adventurer. He simply couldn't stand being bored. One night, he snuck out of his house and ran far away. He ran for days, passed all the cities, farms, and reservoirs, hiding from the BoPo wherever he ran. One time he almost got caught. With the BoPo right on his tail, he hid inside a trouser gopher hole (A trouser gopher is a relative of the pocket gopher but much bigger). The BoPo spent such a long amount of time looking for him, they got bored and forgot what they were doing, so eventually they left. Johnny Muur crept out of the gopher hole and looked around.

'Where in tarnation am I?' he asked.

There was nothing around him. Nothing. Just flat grey dirt as far as the eye could see. He looked in all directions for quite some time. After a few minutes, he noticed that the sun would soon be setting.

'I'd better move on,' he figured, 'but which way should I go? I know I come from that direction... And I ain't going back! Anything is better than being bored for the rest of my life. Johnny squinted far out into the horizon. After a moment, he shrugged his shoulders and said aloud 'I think I'll just go the opposite direction.' Off went Johnny into the sunset.

"This Johnny guy was really brave," said Maggie aloud. She thought for a moment, "I wonder if I would do what he did?" She glanced briefly at the book on her dresser and continued reading.

Johnny walked on the flat grey dirt into the sunset and into the night. The sky was clear. The air was quite. It was going to be a warm night. 'Perfect night for walkin,' thought Johnny. 'It's too dark to see where I'm going. I'll just close my eyes and put one foot in front of the other and see where I end up in the morning.' And that is exactly what he did. He walked on, and on, step, after step, hour, after, hour. It was late in the night when Johnny became very tired, actually, downright exhausted. He wanted to stop and rest, but he didn't want to wake up on the flat grey dirt. He remembered how much there was in front of him when he started out. He wanted to see something special when he opened his eyes. Onward he walked, on the flat grey dirt. His legs were becoming very wobbly. He was becoming very sleepy.

"Must. Keep. Walkin," he uttered. Eventually, his exhaustion was simply unbearable, "Okay (breath). I'm gonna (breath), open my eyes".

Johnny opened his eyes and as he did, he tripped on something with the clip of his heal. It was hard and heavy and unyielding. Johnny lost all balance and fell forward. He remembered falling longer than he should have. 'If all the ground is flat, I should have hit it by now,' he thought.

He must have been on a ledge of some kind. He didn't know how long he had fallen. All he knew is that when he landed he was on his back, laying on soft cool grass. He heard the sound of running water next to him. Before he blacked out, Johnny looked up at the night sky. It was gorgeous. A million stars pierced through the black matte of night. The moon was a bright silvery crescent, and off to one side, he could see the faintest glow of a sunrise. It was the most beautiful sight he had ever seen. Exhaustion took over. He couldn't fight it anymore. Johnny fell asleep.

By this time, Maggie was completely absorbed in what she was reading. She looked up from her laptop and checked the time. "11:30!!!!! Dad is going to kill me!" she thought. "Wait a second, I'm on summer vacation. I'll just read a little longer and then I'll go to bed."

She quickly got up from her desk, walked out into the hall, eyeing the strange book on her dresser as she passed, drank a glass of water, brushed her teeth, and changed into her pj's. "I hope this doesn't take too much longer. I really should get back to researching the Smoky

Grand YellowPark place, or whatever you call it. I am too tired to remember what it's called." She slid into the covers and turned back to reading the story.

Johnny Muur awoke to the sound of humming insects all around him. His legs were stiff. His mouth was parched. He groggily shifted about on the comfortable mat of bunch grass that had served as a bed. When he opened his eyes, it was bright. The sun was high above him. It took a while for him to collect himself. He was thirsty from his travels. He remembered falling asleep to the sound of running water. 'Where is it?' he said.

He sat up and looked behind him only to find a crystal blue river flowing beside him. 'Good thing I didn't land in there.' he said. Johnny rolled over to a kneeling position and dipped his hand in the water and drank from it. It was delicious. Pure and clean. He had never tasted water so good. He drank until he was full.

'Where am I?' he said aloud. That is when he stood up and looked around. 'Golly!' was all he could mutter.

Johnny stood at the edge of a vast valley. The river bordered the immense valley like an arching belt of blue ribbon. The desert of grey dirt that he had traveled across the night before encompassed the river on its outer banks in a wide circular boundary that stretched in both directions as far as the eye could see.

He saw tall snow capped mountains with jagged peaks far in the background. He saw huge canyons in between the peaks. Vast forests, meadows and bluffs spread out on the valley floor. Off to his right, the mountains were smaller and less jagged. They were somewhat clouded over in a blue mist of some kind. To the right, he could see a large lake in the distance surrounded by an expansive plain. He could see large herds of animals feeding on the plain. Then, directly on the other side of the river, steam started to fume out from a mound. The steam got stronger and stronger until water sprayed out. The spray must have been a hundred feet tall. It geysered out of the ground for several minutes, and that was all that Johnny could look at. Eventually, the geyser lost strength and gradually disappeared back underground. That was when Johnny realized he was next to a colorful meadow of wildflowers of blues, reds, yellows and purples. Hummingbirds zipped from flower to flower. He saw something big and brown moving slowly in the middle of the meadow across the river. At first, it looked like a big log, but then, the big log raised its big head. Its big head had an enormous set of antlers.

'That's a moose!' gasped Johnny, 'I thought they went extinct!' The moose saw Johnny and looked at him steadily while it chewed lazily on a large wad of plant greens.

That was the start of something very special. That was the day that Johnny Muur discovered a small portion of what would later become Grand Smoky Yellowsemite National Park. Johnny spent the next few years exploring all the corners of this grand wonderland. He found waterfalls taller than skyscrapers. He found elk, wolves, eagles and bears. All the animals that had disappeared long ago in the country where Johnny was from. He explored its many river gorges and canyons and also found many geysers in the plain surrounding what he called Yellowsemite Lake. He even met an ancient tribe of people who called this majestic land their home. He had many adventures and discovered many great things.

Perhaps his greatest discovery was one that is more fiction than fact. Of all his stories, none is more fascinating than the Legend of the Emerald Trout. 'Purtiest thing I ever did set eyes on' as he put it.

It was on the banks of the river he first stumbled upon: The Flowy River. The Flowy River borders much of the park with the Flat Grey Dirt Desert. It happened on the first morning that Johnny discovered the park. Johnny had landed on the desert side of the river but he desperately wanted to be on the park side. He was walking along the banks, trying to find a safe spot to cross, when something in the water caught his eye. It was a fish, actually the tail of a fish gliding steadily from side to side on the bottom of the gin clear river. It was a big tail too, gracefully rounded and fanned out like a ginkgo leaf, and delicately forked inward in the center. The tail swayed back and forth in the river. Johnny could see the tail, but he couldn't make out the body. He knelt down and peered deeply into the water. He shielded his eyes from the glare of the sun and stared longer. The fish's tail was so rhythmic, Johnny became hypnotized. Then, like a flash of green lightning, the fish moved. All Johnny could see was a burst of emerald green as the fish moved to swallow a nymph drifting passed its snout.

'It's a trout… Got to be three feet long!' gasped Johnny. 'Golly Gee! That sure is purdy!'

He watched the trout for several hours hoping to get a full view of it. The trout was magical. It completely blended in with the rocky river bottom when at rest. But whenever it opened its mouth to eat, the sun would reflect off of it and the trout would light up the entire river with a brilliant emerald green color.

As the day wore on, the food the trout had been feeding on had changed. It wasn't feeding on underwater larvae anymore. In fact, as Johnny saw it, the trout wasn't feeding at all. The fish hadn't moved for several minutes and Johnny was beginning to get hungry. He was just getting up from the riverbank to look for some food when something soft brushed against his nose. Johnny stepped back quickly.

It was a mayfly. And a big one at that. With it legs spread out, it was the size of his palm. The mayfly fluttered past him and slowly descended onto the flowing water. Once it hit the water, it stayed motionless as it floated with the current. It had big clear wings that pointed to the sky. Its six legs touched the water and made dimples on the surface. The body was a woody brown color. Something brushed against Johnny's ear, another mayfly. It also glided gently onto the river. Then another one landed, and another one. Within a minute the sky was clouded with giant brown mayflies, all landing on the water. There had to be thousands of them. Again Johnny was mesmerized.

'It's snowing, mayflies!' Johnny chuckled in disbelief.

He watched the armada of brown creatures sail downstream. Suddenly one of the bugs disappeared under the water with a green flash. Then another disappeared with a green flash.

'That there trout is feeding on those mayflies,' said Johnny.

Another one disappeared but this time the trout raised part of its body out of the water. Johnny was blinded by its green brilliance.

'Hey, I can't see nothin, dadgumit!' Johnny rubbed his eyes for quite some time before his vision began to return. He could hear the trout splashing about in the water as it dined on its winged feast. As his eyesight recovered, the sky had darkened. He looked up to see that a small cloud had covered the sun. Johnny was a little nervous when he turned to look back at the river. The mayflies no longer filled the air and most had drifted far downstream. They had disappeared as quickly as they had arrived. There were only a handful of them that were still close by. He looked for the trout. It was no longer on the bottom. Had it followed the mass of mayflies farther downstream? No.

Once again, Johnny found the tail underneath his very feet and the grassy undercut bank he was standing on. 'I bet I could reach it,' Johnny thought as he licked his lips.

'I'm having trout for dinner tonight.' Johnny inched his hand closer to the waterline. The tail swayed hypnotically. Johnny's fingertips touched the pure, mountain water. It was cold, but it made him feel alive. He could feel the power of the river as it flowed between his fingers. 'I have to be quick,' thought Johnny. 'Can't miss, gotta grab tight cuz she's gonna fight me' Johnny moved his wrist into the water. He was within striking distance. 'One, Two,' The tail stopped swaying, 'Three!' Johnny lunged his arm into the water. He clenched his hand where the trout had been.

And grabbed nothing.

'Aww sassafras,' muttered Johnny. He looked up to see the last mayfly float by him. 'Looks like it's just you and me bud,' said a defeated and hungry Johnny.

And then "SPLASH!" The trout thundered out of the water, mayfly in its jaw. It leapt clear out of the water, showing its magnificent, lightning green body for all the world to see. The moment passed by in slow motion to Johnny. He could see the trout thrash its body from side to side. With the sun clouded over, he could now see the trout clearly. It was a dark brown with elegant marbling. Bolts of electric green coursed between the thin lines of marbling. The bolts flashed and surged in all directions like a lightning storm.

'That must be how it lights up,' gasped Johnny.

Water dripped from its sleek, shiny body. It was quite simply, the most beautiful thing imaginable. The trout began to fall back to the water. It turned its body away from the sky and back towards its watery home. As it did so, it pointed its head back towards Johnny. Johnny stared at the fish. The descending fish stared back. And then it did something that Johnny never could understand. Something that Johnny would spend his entire life trying to understand. Just before the trout dove back under, it winked at Johnny. The trout winked at Johnny and disappeared back into the crystal blue water.

It took Johnny a long time to recover from that experience. He replayed the moment in his head time and time again, but he just couldn't explain it. He spent a little more time that day trying to find the trout, but eventually his hunger got the better of him and he was forced to move on. He never did find that fish again. Although he returned many times to where he thought he had seen it, he just couldn't find it. He never forgot about it through all of his adventures.

After five years of adventure, Johnny had explored almost all of what would later end up being protected as National Park land. He had just given up another fruitless visit to the Flowy River to look for the emerald trout when Johnny realized something very important. He stopped dead in his tracks and stared ahead, deep in thought, 'I've been gone for so long, they must be lookin' for me.' He looked far out over the land in front of him, 'What if somebody else finds this place?' he thought. 'What will they do?' He paced around fiercely, recalling what the world looked like where he had come from. He stopped abruptly as he contemplated a horrifying realization. 'They'll surely come here and do what they did to all the other wild places. It'll just turn into more farms, and cities, and reservoirs.' Johnny stood silently, like a statue, running the dreadful scenario through his mind. He exhaled weakly and collapsed upon his knees, grasping the lush, innocent meadow grass beneath him tightly in his hands. He clutched the gentle blades between his fingers firmly, as if they were the only things keeping him from sliding off of a cliff.

Johnny looked at the wild and free earth beneath him. He began to breath heavily as though he had just finished running a marathon. He spoke aloud, 'I can't let that happen here. It's too special. It's gotta to be protected," he stammered 'I gotta go back, I gotta tell 'em... that we can't treat this place the same way we done treated everywhere else. It's too special... It's too special.'

That is when Johnny Muur came up with a brilliant idea. 'Grand Smoky Yellowsemite National Park! A place where everyone can visit and what is special will always be.' Johnny stood up, crossed the river, climbed up its steep desert bank and walked straight back to his nearly forgotten home, across the Flat Grey Dirt Desert, passed all the farms and cities and reservoirs. He went straight to his house and wrote down all of his adventures. He worked feverishly to recount all his stories, spending five whole days, writing day and night, recalling all his tales. When he had finished, he went to the governor's home and personally delivered his stories to the governor. The governor looked a little surprised to see him so Johnny went back home to await the governor's response.

At first the governor didn't know what to think about Johnny. All of a sudden, here's this dirty, smelly man who looked like he had been in a wrestling match with a dust devil, claiming to have found the most beautiful place on earth, so beautiful that it need to be protected. 'Very strange,' thought the governor, 'I've never heard of such a notion, but I might as well glance at his writings'.

Eventually the governor got around to reading Johnny's stories and by the end of the first page, he was in awe. 'If this place truly does exist, we must protect it!' he shouted. The governor then called the president and sent him Johnny's stories. The president read the stories and also agreed that such a place deserved protection.

'Let's have Johnny show us around this place,' said the president to the governor. They called Johnny to tell him the good news, but Johnny wasn't home. He had left his house weeks before. They had called Johnny's house. His answering machine picked up, 'Hi! This is Johnny, I'm sorry I'm not home. I won't be comin home neither. I've left to go back to Yellowsemite. I need to see that trout one last time, so don't leave a message, 'cause I won't be returning. Thanks. Bye. Johnny had gone straight back to the wilderness of Grand Smoky Yellowsemite and was never heard from again. Most importantly though, the president and governor kept their promise. They toured Yellowsemite together and immediately made it a National Park: The first National Park.

This is how Yellowsemite became a National Park.

Maggie had finished reading the web page, yet she still stared at the computer screen for a while after. She didn't move. She just sat there, in her bed, deep in thought. Finally, she relaxed her posture, looked up from her screen and, under her breath, murmured, "Okay... Grand Smoky Yellowsemite National Park. Might be fun." She closed the laptop and tossed it to the side of her bed, reached to the wall switch and turned off the lights. Maggie had researched enough for one night. It was time to sleep.

CHAPTER

3

The days that followed went by very fast for Maggie. As one might expect, she kept herself very busy researching everything she could about her upcoming family project (something most would call a vacation). Maggie felt that the bigger a project was, the more she needed to research. For Maggie, Grand Smoky Yellowsemite was about as big as it got. She soon realized that she did not have enough time to get all the facts.

"This just isn't going to work," she said to herself defeatedly. Maggie promptly left her room and went into the garage where her father was organizing camping supplies. "We need to push back the deadline," she blurted.

Father looked up from a dusty worn box marked 'camp cooking.' "Excuse me?" he asked skeptically.

"We need to push back our departure time, I'm not going to be ready." answered Maggie.

"Ready for what Maggie?" asked Father incredulously.

"YELLOWSEMITE DAD!!! What else would I be talking about?" she stammered.

He looked at her curiously, and dropped his jaw a little, trying to understand what the real issue was. After a pause he asked "Are you, starting, woman stuff?"

"No DAD! I'm trying to tell you there is too much information that I need to find about this place. I can't find anything on the bison migratory paths, or anything on the wooly mammoth captive breeding program... I can't find one smidge of information about this supposed emerald trout. What am I supposed to do Dad?" said Maggie emphatically.

It was moments like these when Maggie's Father really missed Maggie's Mother. Maggie was like her in so many ways. The way she looked standing at the door, hands at her hips, nostrils flared, her cheeks just the faintest bit rosy. Her Mother would have been so proud. He suddenly began to miss his wife, but collected himself lest he show Maggie any sign of his inner struggles.

"Sweetheart, the world can't stop for us. We have to use the time that is given to us and make the most of it. I know that you want to be prepared for anything while we are away, but you can't be fully prepared. You have to go with what you have and trust that it is enough," said Father as gracefully as he could.

Maggie wanted to say something. Something smart. Something that proved her point better, but she couldn't. She knew he was right. "Ughh," she mumbled in defeat.

As she turned to leave, he asked, "Maggie?"

She turned back around, shoulders hunched over, her head drooped forward like a sad little vulture "What?" she responded.

"Have you packed? You know we are leaving first thing tomorrow." he reminded.

Maggie placed her hands on her hips and squinted up towards the ceiling as she ran off her list of luggage, "Umm, well I have all the maps and field guides ready. I have my GPS and compass. I have my butterfly net, fishing pole for catching lizards, binoculars, royal pheasant mating call, an ice ax for glissading. I have one hundred feet of paracord, a twelve inch bowie knife, a vile of mountain diamondback rattlesnake antivenom-with i.v kit, umm 120 piece medica......"

"Maggie!" interrupted Father. "Do you have any clothes packed? That's what I meant. Do you plan on using clothes while you're away?"

"Ohhh! Uhhh, well I guess I should probably pack some clothes," she replied.

"Yes Sweetie. They might come in handy," advised Father.

"Yes Dad, I'm sure they will." Again she turned to go back inside the house, but she remembered one last thing to tell the man. She smiled in reflection and turned around slowly once more, "Ya know, Dad? I think I'm really excited."

Father looked up from his preparations and smiled at her fondly.

CHAPTER

4

$\mathcal{B}$y the time the first rays of morning sunlight shone through the dusty blinds of Maggie's bedroom window, Maggie had showered, brushed her teeth and hair, eaten breakfast and was waiting in the living room with all her luggage neatly stacked by the front door. After exactly ten minutes of waiting she walked into the kitchen, grabbed her father's "#1 Dad" coffee mug from the dish rack and filled it to the brim with Cousin Lefty's Instant MochaCapaFrapaLataCino. Then, without spilling, walked into his room to wake him up with coffee in bed.

What ensued next were the typical shenanigans that occur when anyone embarks on a family vacation for the first time in a long while. Piping hot coffee gets spilled numerous times. The groggy parent is slow to get out of bed and can't find glasses. Daughter finds them. Bad morning breath. Bathroom duties and dressing. Daughter waits in living room. Finally, said parent is ready to start loading vehicle. Backs car out of garage into driveway. Transfer luggage from inside of house to outside onto moist lawn. Realize that A: the car is too small, or B: too much luggage has been packed. Father tries to fill car anyways. No good. Try again. No good. Daughter tries to help. Father asks her to wait and be patient. Father tries again. No good. Daughter begins to get irritated at Father. Father also irritated with himself gives the, 'Don't say one word' stare to daughter. Father tries one last time. Success! More or less. Lock all doors to house. Check windows. Close Garage door. And off they go! Down the city streets, headed towards the interstate, and eventually, to Yellowsemite.

Maggie and her father felt quite victorious as they left their sleepy, sub-urban neighborhood. They felt ready for the road. Father had a full cup of coffee in an insulated, spill proof container. He also had an entire travel mix of music ready for any event the road could conjure. Maggie was equally prepared. She had an entire workstation fashioned around her. She had overtaken the glove compartment with snacks and books. The map compartment had been filled with, maps. On the floorboard sat a stuffed backpack filled with various, vital travel resources. Yes they were ready.

They turned onto old, familiar city streets. Father sat in the driver's seat humming to himself, "On the road again... I just can't wait to get back on the road again."

Maggie sat alertly in the passenger seat, her excitement was almost over-flowing. She could not wait to see the entrance gates of Yellowsemite. Those gates were a long distance away from her at the moment. Maggie was okay with that knowledge. She repeated the conversation she had with her father about getting bored along the way, "We'll just make an adventure out of it. Find big things within the little things."

Maggie looked promisingly at the sights around her. She had seen these city streets before. She had already traveled on them a hundred times since birth. She was used to their sounds and smells, and would nor-mally dismiss them along with the everyday sights. She knew these streets well enough to dismiss them. They always looked the same. They often bored her, but today was different.

She couldn't help but take interest in all the routine happenings. Her excitement made everything more interesting. For the first time, she took interest in the city she lived in. She could smell that Newman's Bakery had just taken its famous french sourdough out of the ovens as they motored by the storefront. Her father's spaghetti was always better with a fresh slice of Newman's french sourdough, so light and fluffy, and doughy.

They turned onto bustling Market Street. The mid morning sun shone brightly down in between the tall buildings that lined the street. Maggie looked at the facial expressions of the people walking on the clean, wide sidewalk. Crisp sunlight highlighted the facial expressions of the pedestrians. Some looked happy, some looked tired. Some looked busy and some looked confident. Others were talking and some looked nervous. She could see a story in each person she looked at. She wanted to know more about the people in her city. For the first time, she wanted to know more about the city she lived in. It is amazing what a little excitement can spark.

As they drove away from the city center, and towards the outskirts, they entered the industrial portion of the city. Maggie had never enjoyed driving through this area. Industrial sectors are often dirty and grimey. Steam puffs out overhead from cold, concrete stacks. Weird smells emanate out of nowhere. And there are no trees to be found here. It is pavement and factories. Red brick walls and chain link fencing. Industry is production. Production rules over all. Anything else is a waste. There are no soft edges. There is no need for comfort in industry and this industrial area was no different. Even here, Maggie's excitement kept her entertained. She read the logo of one of the passing buildings.

"Look Dad! It's Wild Tech Industries! I didn't know we had one here! They made my boots, and my ice axe, and my paracord," she shouted. "Oh man, I would love to get a job there!"

Father was surprised and pleased to hear Maggie take interest in a getting a job, but did not want his enthusiasm to show through. "What happened to wanting to be a detective? And ASB Club, and volleyball, and water polo? How are you going to make time for all of your pursuits?" he poked.

"I don't know Dad... I'll figure it out," she answered back. She watched the building fade away from view in the side mirror. "Interesting," speaking to herself. "I wonder how long Wild Tech has been here? I never noticed them before. Maybe because I didn't know what Wild Tech was a week ago," she chuckled aloud. Father glanced at Maggie proudly. Maggie let out a sigh of content. She returned to watching the buildings pass by. "I wonder what they do in all these other buildings?" she pondered.

It wasn't long before they were out of the industry, past the city limits, and out onto the highway. The open road, where things pass by faster. Where the earth gets flat. Where the farms are. After a few hours of driving father invited conversation over the monotony of highway sounds. "This is farmland Maggie," said Father. "This is where all of the food we eat comes from."

Maggie was immersed in reading Johnny Muur's book. She lifted her head up. "Cool!" she remarked. She looked out the window on her father's side, then to the front, and then to her side. All she could see in any direction were crops. Rows of tall green plants whizzed by along the highway side. Every once in awhile a red dirt road would emerge from, and then quickly disappear into, tall stands of plants. Maggie watched this sight for many miles. It didn't take long before she started to get bored. She thought about Johnny Muur running through these very fields, being chased by the BoPo.

"Dad?" Maggie asked.

"Yes Sweetie?" responded Father.

"It's all the same out here. It's just crops. I haven't seen a farmer, or even a house. I thought you said this was farmland. Where's all the farmers?" implored Maggie.

Father listened intently and then answered, "Well Maggie, that is a good question," he paused. "I guess it's just the point we're at right now in the world. There are a lot of people on this planet. And every person needs to eat. I guess this is the best place to grow food. I don't think anyone intended for it to look the same. This is just the easiest way to feed everyone. There are other kinds of crops that are grown. Just not here, and they grow lots of those too. There are still farmers and farmhouses, just not as many as there used to be. Most of the farms are owned by big corporations now. Most of the work is done by machine. They just don't need many farmers to do the job."

"I did not imagine farms to be like this," replied Maggie.

"I don't think anyone did Maggie. It wasn't this way when I was kid. It just sort of happened," responded Father reluctantly.

Maggie decided to let the issue rest. She stared out at the rows of crops on both sides of the road ahead.

"Dad?" asked Maggie in a very particular tone.

Father knew that tone. He had used that tone with his parents when he was a boy traveling over long distances. Every parent knows that tone. Because everyone asks that question at least once in their life.

"Yes Maggie?" said Father.

"Are we there yet?" she asked, trying not to whine.

"Hahaha," chuckled Father. "You lasted longer than I did on my first road trip. Well we are making good time, but I think you already know that we are nowhere near Yellowsemite. You were just looking at your maps. I bet you know exactly how far away we are."

"I do," said Maggie solemnly. "We're about 1,200 miles away…"

"Well then Maggie, I'd say we're about 1,200 miles away," answered Father humorously.

Maggie was not as amused.

Father attempted to pacify the situation, "Look on the bright side. We're about halfway through with the farmland, and if we're lucky, tomorrow we will drive along the banks of the reservoirs. After that it's the Flat Grey Dirt Desert. And then Yellowsemite. Plus, it's getting late in the afternoon and we'll need to get gas. We'll stop soon." Maggie eyed him skeptically.

They travelled peacefully across the monotonous agrarian landscape for a couple hours longer. The once clear blue sky had now lost all azure. It was mostly a greenish yellow. A few large dark clouds blocked the low hanging sun. Below the smooth clouds cast a dark orange haze with a maroon red band on the horizon. It was the makings of a very pleasant evening.

Maggie had not even seen a building since they had left the outskirts of the city. She did not believe in her father's confidence that lodging, let alone a gas station, even existed out in this unvarying land of plant productivity. Yet sure enough, after a short while longer, a large lit up billboard emerged in the distance against a darkening sky. As they drove closer Maggie could read its message, "*Gas, Food, Lodging*".

"See Maggie. Told you," said Father.

Father signaled with his blinker and gently slowed the car down. The experience quickly became much quieter. Maggie had not noticed how loud the sound of the highway was while traveling at cruise speed. Father pulled off of the empty highway. The momentary peaceful quiet was quickly replaced by the crunchy sound of rubber tires on gravel. Father strolled the car into the empty parking lot, pulled it into a vacant space and turned off the engine. Maggie unclasped her seatbelt, opened her door and crunched onto the gravel.

It was balmy and warm outside. Maggie instantly heard a distinctly familiar sound. A sound that she had often heard walking to and from school. It was the harmonious hum of many insects, except they weren't cicadas in trees, they were grasshoppers in the fields. There had to be thousands of them. They buzzed and chattered and hopped amongst the crops around her. They were surprisingly loud. Their song was very harmonic. The sound of their legs rubbing against each other vibrated in Maggie's ear and resonated peacefully.

"Neat," said a road tired Maggie. She paused for a moment to take in her new surroundings and pay homage to the symphony of hoppers. She heard her father's door close and the sound of footsteps walking away. She turned to see Father walking towards the lodge. Maggie grabbed her backpack from the floorboard, closed the car door and followed him inside.

Once inside the main lobby, with doors closed, the buzzing bugs were barely audible above the steady groan of an air conditioner. Noisy gravel that clung to the rubber soles of tennis shoes was swiftly brushed away by firm carpeting. Maggie's father spoke to the receptionist at the counter. Maggie paid no mind to the transaction and instead explored and contemplated her surroundings. She had never stayed in a place that did not belong to a family member or friend. Everything was bland and inconspicuous. Nothing was out of order. Nothing was remarkable. Her surroundings were very bland. Again she thought of Johnny and his quest for adventure.

"Come along Maggie," said Father breaking her concentration. She followed him around the corner and down a long hallway to a nondescript door that resembled all the other doors in the hallway. The only difference with this door was the number centered above it. Maggie looked around noticing that every other door had a different number as well. So even their differences made them the same. Father unlocked the door and stepped inside. Maggie followed.

The buzzing sound of the crickets had a calming effect on Maggie. She could hear them inside her hotel room. Here she was, in the middle of farmland. A place she had never been before, that did not make much sense to her, but the knowledge that this foreign land also harbored familiar things made her feel much more at ease. She never expected to have to sleep in a strange place. It can be hard to do, but the notion didn't really bother her with the familiar sounds of buzzing bugs outside her window. She knew that the mattress she would sleep on would not be as comfortable as her's at home, but that didn't matter either. She knew that if she had any difficulties falling asleep, all she would need to do is open a window and listen to the sound of being back home.

CHAPTER

5

*A*s it turns out, Maggie had no trouble falling asleep. She awoke just as alert and bright eyed as she had the day before, ready to go, ready for adventure. Father was a little bit faster at getting ready this time around. They ate an unremarkable breakfast of cold zucchini pancakes, kangaroo paws, and a few slices of muskmelon. With stomachs relatively satisfied, they paid for their lodging and returned to their car. When Maggie stepped out onto the gravel, it was already surprisingly warm. The sun was very bright and she shielded her eyes to avoid being blinded.

"It's gonna be a hot one," said Father reluctantly. "We better fill up and get back to the highway." So they did.

Once again the tires crunched over the gravel and sailed quickly onto the open road. Not much had changed since they were last on the highway. The only difference was that Father turned on the swamp cooler to keep the cab from getting too warm inside. The setting had not changed. Still nothing but row crops as far as the eye could see.

"Umm, Dad? I think I'm going to read until we get a change of scenery," said Maggie trying to pacify her boredom.

"Go right on ahead," said Father in stride. "I hope you don't mind. I'm going to play some music."

"Sure Dad," responded Maggie.

Maggie reached into the glove box and pulled out Johnny's book. Her eyes flashed with excitement as she ran her fingers over the worn cover. She fondly placed the book to her nose. For some odd reason she loved the musky smell of too much time spent in a cramped and dusty box. She ran her fingertip along the bent crease that scarred the cover. It was soft and fibrous like cotton and revealed its frail composition. She loved the feel of its gritty, yet feathery pages on her fingers. She loved reading the book even more.

She opened it up. Within an instant Maggie was transported from the monotonous, neverending rows of green she was driving through, to the adventurous realm of Mr. Muur. She was now standing at the foot of a thunderous waterfall, hiking a craggy, desolate ridgeline, and laying in a meadow watching firestars fall from a crisp, clear night sky. What incredible experiences were bound in this book. More dreamlike than real. Maggie was transfixed… spellbound.

She read intently as the row crops blurred by. She was deaf to the car stereo twanging out rockabilly tunes from her father's music mix. Maggie was in a different place, in a different time. She was no longer reading words printed on pages. She was right there with Johnny, exploring with him, side by side.

They stood on the top of a grassy knoll, in the center of Yellowsemite Valley. The view was sublime. The sky was clear and the air was temperate. A herd of massive wooly mammoths were grazing beneath a grove of stargazer lily trees nearby. The air was filled with the tree's sweet scent. One mammoth in the front of the herd bore a furry coat that hung longer than the rest. Its tusks were also much larger than the others.

"That's Edgar," said Johnny to Maggie. "He's the herd leader. Oldest of the clan. Reigns over this valley."

They stood silently, watching the herd from their verdant vantage point for some time until Edgar stopped grazing and lifted his head. His massive shaggy body stood motionless. He could hear something. Johnny and Maggie watched in captivation. Edgar swung his massive head to one side and listened intently. With one loud solemn snort from his trunk, he signaled it was time for the herd to move on. It was surprising how fast the herd cleared the area. Their thunderous steps could be heard, and then felt, long after they had vacated.

Out of nowhere, a cold breeze started to blow from the north. It was shockingly chilly and it did not pause. Maggie no longer wanted to sight-see. She wanted warmth, and shelter.

"Paradise has its price," chuckled Johnny.

Maggie looked at Johnny. His clothes were completely saturated, as if he had been dunked in a swimming pool. Water droplets dripped onto the grass at his feet. His long frizzy beard and old canvas hat weighed down with water. He must have been freezing but he showed no sign to Maggie. He only looked at her fondly, his squinty eyes sparkled, a warm smile emerged from his coarse facial hair.

Maggie shivered at the sight of him. She was quite uncomfortable and no longer interested in exploring with Johnny. At that moment the sun became blocked. She shielded her eyes and looked up to see what the source of the shade was. Johnny also looked up. At first it was not apparent to Maggie as to what was blocking the sun. There was an object, but it was not a cloud. It had a distinct outline. It floated motionless, high above the two spectators. It was large, whatever it was.

"Oh boy…" said Johnny. "That's a… That's…."

"What is it?" implored Maggie.

"That! Is an eagle! An emperor eagle! Biggest bunch of feathers you ever did set eyes on," he answered absently.

Maggie could now make out its outline. It was indeed an enormous bird. She could see its colossal, outstretched wings, and broad, fanned out tail. It was a very dark bird, charcoal grey, nearly black. It hovered high above them in the frigid, breezy sky, stationary, like a puppet hanging on a string.

"Kerrrrreeeeeeeeeeeeeee," the eagle screached from high above.

Maggie squinted harder, focused only on the beastly bird. At that moment the eagle closed its wings and began to dive. It looked as if it was diving right at them.

"Oh my!" alerted Maggie. She gasped in fear. She had never seen an eagle before, let alone an eagle diving, but she knew what was happening. The eagle was about to attack its prey.

"What do we do?" trembled Maggie.

Johnny turned once more to Maggie with the same warm, estranged smile. His wrinkle shrouded, squinty eyes glistened like black obsidian. He did not appear the least bit concerned of the impending danger. Water sheeted off of him like water sheeting down oily asphalt during a downpour. If Maggie had not been preoccupied by the notion that she was about to become a meal, she would have held more concern for her friend's peculiar condition.

"Johnny! What do we do?" cried Maggie.

"Kerrrrreeeeeeeeeeeeeeeeeeeeeeeeee," the eagle called again but was much louder, closer.

Maggie turned once more to the sky. She could now clearly see the eagle. It was a tremendous creature. Even with its wings folded, it was the size of a car. And it was a dark creature. No light reflected off of its feathers. Only the beak and talons had any color, a bright yellow. The winged beast was careening right onto Maggie. It's body becoming larger as it descended from the sky.

There was nowhere to run. She had nothing to defend herself with. The eagle was upon her. As it overtook her, the eagle spread out its lofty wings to slow its descent. It outstretched sharp yellow talons towards Maggie. She could hear the powerful "swoosh" of air being displaced by the flap of feathers that were the length of her arm as the bird opened up its massive wings to stop its descent. She could now see the eyes of the predator. They were fixed on her. The eagle's stare was as blank as Johnny's. There was no mercy in its gaze, no consolation. Maggie's mortality was of no concern to the animal.

The monstrous animal overtook Maggie like a child with a rag doll. It now had Maggie within its grasp. It tightened its talons around her and pressed her body to the ground. Maggie wanted to yell. She wanted to scream, to signal to Johnny to save her. She looked at him one last time in a plea for help. Her innocent eyes pleaded for mercy, for freedom.

"The river gives, and the river takes," said Johnny. He spoke as if he was a judge delivering a 'guilty verdict' to a seasoned criminal.

"What?" squealed Maggie. "What does that have to do with what is happening right now?" she pleaded.

Johnny stared back blankly. Water poured off of him as though he stood underneath a waterfall. The eagle had Maggie completely restrained. She was pinned tightly in place by its scaly claws. The bird began to beat its broad wings to get airborne. Maggie's stomach dropped at the shear force of lift off. The eagle gave one last giant flap of its wings and she was aloft. Maggie's heart pounded in fear. Each powerful wingbeat lifted her higher above the grassy knoll. Each forceful wingbeat drained her of consciousness. Maggie was tucked securely within the eagle's dark feathers. For a moment, Maggie's overwhelming fear caused her to black out, and in the blink of an eye, the eagle had vanished.

In an instant, Maggie was once again standing with Johnny. He was wearing the same tattered clothes as before, but he was no longer soaking wet. He was completely dry. Maggie looked about to understand her surroundings. She and Johnny were on the banks of the Flowy River. Maggie had her back to the icy, churning water. Terrified and confused, she tried to run away, but couldn't. Something was holding her back. She tried to wiggle free. The grip tightened. It was the eagle. She couldn't see it but see she could feel it. The bird's talons held her tightly like a mummy, embalmed in a dead man's cloth. Johnny stared at Maggie and the river behind her.

"The river gives, and the river takes," said Johnny once more. He was just as cold and accusing as ever.

Maggie's body began to get pulled out over the water. Johnny stood motionless on the bank, watching Maggie helplessly, like an engaged spectator watching a horror film at a theatre. Maggie tried to struggle against the invisible force that was taking her, but couldn't. She could feel the talons of the eagle still around her as it pulled her out, and into the water. It was the same feeling she experienced when the eagle first embraced her. She could breath, but there was no escaping its grasp.

It pulled her out to the middle of the frigid river. Maggie was overcome with fear. All she could do was look at Johnny on the bank. Maggie was now being drug into the water. She was not able to tilt her head but she could see the wake her body made as it was forcibly submerged. Johnny stared on.

Maggie could feel the water. It wasn't cold. It wasn't warm. It felt more like a pressure being pushed against her body. Deeper and deeper into the water she was pulled. She could feel the pressure of the water at her shoulders, now her neck, now her mouth. She looked helplessly across the river to Johnny. Johnny only smiled back and waved farewell. She closed her eyes as she was drug under.

With her eyes closed she could see nothing but bright green light. It was actually very calming and peaceful. She could feel the pressure of the water all around her. It pressed against her skin, and whispered sweet nothings. She was now completely under water. After waiting a moment,

Maggie had not suffered any. She wasn't drowning. She decided to open her eyes. She counted silently, "One. Two. Three."

Maggie opened her eyes to find herself sitting comfortably in the passenger seat of her car. *A Special Land* had fallen at her feet and she could feel that there was dried saliva on her right cheek. She wiped it aggressively with the back of her hand.

"You fell asleep Sweetie," greeted her Father.

"Umm," looking around wildly, "I guess I did." Maggie stretched about in her seat. "What on earth just happened?" Maggie thought to herself, "I know that we've been driving this whole time but that dream was way too real." She looked about frantically to ensure that she wasn't still being haunted by that madman Johnny Muur. Her heart pounded stressfully. Her body wanted to jump out of its skin. She had never been so uncomfortable in her life. Maggie gripped her knees tightly with her hands. She fidgeted about in her seat.

"What does it mean?" she thought to herself. Maggie tried to relax and let out a shaky breath. She eased her body back into its seat, and looked out of the window to see if they had made any progress.

Rubbing her face to shake the anxiety "Umm" she sounded, "the crops are different. And we're in the hills too." She pressed her face against the window pane to get a better view. "Ouch! That window is hot!" she retracting painfully away from the glass.

"Yeah Sweetie, That's because it's about 110 degrees outside. I guess the sun decided to come out and join us while you had your little catnap," responded Father nonchalantly.

It certainly was hot. The view had improved from earlier in the day. They were now traveling through gentle, rolling hills. The crops a little more interesting than before. These plants had rough, dark green leaves. Each plant grew into a different shape. Each shape was vaguely familiar to her. She couldn't put a finger on it though.

"How long was I out for?" asked Maggie. Still unsure if she had actually been asleep.

Father scratched his head, "Oh, I'd say about 2 hours."

"Wow, I don't remember falling asleep. I was reading my book. And then… It felt like I was in the book." Maggie absently drifted back into her nightmarish thoughts.

She then proceeded to tell her father about her, so called, dream and how real it felt. Father listened intently but did not appear concerned about how real the dream may have seemed. He nodded in recognition and would throw out an occasional 'ohh' or 'aww'. Maggie could not understand if she had really experienced the ordeal or if she had only dreamt it. She watched her father judiciously for clues of disbelief. When she had finished orating her experience, Maggie could see that he was not worried in the least. She decided not to push the matter. "Looks like I'm on my own on this one," thought Maggie. The car fell quiet. She briskly stowed the book back into the glove box and tried to forget the unexplainable experience that had just besieged her.

Maggie stared out at the the conveyor belt of foliage running alongside the highway. The plants were still in uniform rows, but each plant was uncharacteristically unique. Dark green leaves, coarsely textured, grew out in odd clumps. Maggie furrowed her brow in concentration trying to distinguish each individual from the next. "So what kind of crops are these Dad?" asked Maggie after a long pause.

"That's dinosaur kale. Full of vitamins and look at all the shapes it grows into," answered Father.

"Dinosaur kale?" Maggie repeated. She focused in on one passing plant in particular, "Hey, that one looks like a miniature Stegosaurus! And that one looks like a Pterodactyl! And there's a Triceratops!" enamored, Maggie looked out at the crops. In the space of a mile, Maggie identified a handful of dinosaurs that had been discovered to roam the earth millions of years ago.

"Yes, this plant certainly does live up to its name," said Father plainly. Apparently he had already been well accustomed to the plants odd physical characteristics. "We are almost to the reservoirs. Shouldn't be too long now," he said, changing the subject.

Maggie was a little disappointed that he did not seem impressed by the dinosaur kale nor her extremely realistic dream, but the change of scenery was good for her. They traveled across vast fields of prehistoric plants. She tried to identify each species, but there were far too many. As mid-day drifted into early afternoon, she was not as worried about her ominous dream anymore (although it was still in the back of her mind). The excitement of the road and the thrill of adventure had returned her back to high spirits. The vast miles of farmland were gradually beginning to change.

The gently rolling hills eventually lost their gentleness and were replaced with more rugged terrain. Crops no longer covered both sides of the highway. They became more and more intermittent. Rocky outcroppings and small, steep ledges began to mix in with the row crops. She could see little colonies of pocket gophers claiming the rocky outcroppings and ledges as their domain. They would scurry about clumsily for cover as the car whooshed by. It was quite a humorous sight because there was always one chubby gopher standing guard on the highest point of the pocket gopher's territory. It would see the car and alert the rest of the colony by jumping up and down repeatedly. All the other gophers would look up to see and then instantly lose all self control. The smart ones would run and hide for cover, but others did not. They would run around in circles or flail about frantically. Some would roll around on the ground. She saw two especially dimwitted individuals run straight into each other, head on, and knock themselves out cold. All the while, the chubby one jumped up and down above them. "What silly little creatures," thought Maggie, as she laughed uncontrollably.

Before too long, the farms were only on the tops of the hills, where it was flat. The land was becoming increasingly dry. In between the hilltops were steep gullies and washes. Dry scrubby bushes clung to the steep slopes of the gullies. The bottoms were sandy or rocky or a combination of the two. Very few plants grew on the bottom. Maggie could see garbage though. Refrigerators, tires, mattresses, all kinds of waste, littered the floors of the ravines and gullies.

"Why doesn't anything grow here?" Maggie asked.

"Where? Down in the bottom?" Father glanced at Maggie for affirmation, "Ohh, well the bottoms flood in the springtime. You see, there is a very high mountain range a ways to the north of us. Winter storms usually fill the peaks with snow. When temperatures warm up in the spring, the snow melts and floods through these ravines."

That made sense to Maggie. "So why is there so much garbage?" she asked coldly.

Father grumbled a little upon hearing the question, "Well Maggie, there are two reasons why trash is out here. One reason is because people pull off the highway here and dump their garbage illegally. The other reason is because some of the people living at the base of the mountains leave their garbage in their backyards. When the winter storms hit, the wind and the rain and the snow carry the trash downstream."

"Sounds irresponsible," stated Maggie.

"I agree," said Father.

Maggie thought about his answer for a moment. "Well somebody should clean it up," she said at last.

"I agree," said Father.

CHAPTER

6

They drove on, through the increasingly dry terrain, into the afternoon. The summer sun beat down on the intrepid travelers. It was now the hottest part of the day. Even with the swamp cooler running, Maggie could feel heat radiating from the roof of the car. Maggie wanted to slink down in her seat to escape the oppressive sensation. The dark asphalt of the highway looked like it was melting, sending vapors high off of the ground. Although the road was straight, the intense heat made the painted lines on the road move in an "S" like fashion. On more than one occasion Maggie thought she had seen a large animal cross the highway in the distance. She alerted Father.

"That's a mirage Maggie," he said. "When it's hot like this, the mind thinks it sees things that aren't actually there. It plays tricks."

"My mind has been playing tricks on me all day," she said jokingly.

They both chuckled at Maggie's witty joke. But Maggie didn't laugh because she thought she was funny. She laughed to try and ease her looming apprehension. She had been able to return to enjoying the drive, but she couldn't help but think about the terrifying experience she had earlier.

"It was so real," she thought, "I WAS there. There is no way I was dreaming." Maggie wondered if visiting Yellowsemite was such a good idea.

She looked outside to change the mood of her thoughts. It was dry outside. There were very few plants, mainly rough, jagged boulder piles and bare earth. It looked more like the surface of the moon than any place on earth. There were no longer any farms within view. Just a vast, vapory view of asphalt, boulder piles and bare, monolithic earth.

The car traveled across one more extremely steep ravine and then the highway lead them onto an immense uphill grade. It wasn't very steep, but it was definitely uphill. Maggie's ears popped. Maggie leaned forward in her seat to try and see where the crest of the road was. She couldn't see it.

Father knew what Maggie was looking for, "We are almost to The Great Summit Maggie. This is where the farmland ends and where the reservoirs begin."

Maggie was indeed trying to find The Great Summit. She had read a little bit about it when she was researching the route to Yellowsemite. "What did the article say?" She recalled, *"The farthest view and sharpest drop in the world?"* She tapped her fingers against her chin, trying to recall the information.

"We'll reach it soon enough. You'll see," said Father.

Maggie relaxed back in her seat and returned to sightseeing. She was surprised at how quickly the land was transformed as the road traveled higher and higher up the flat, ascending terrain. As they traveled higher in altitude, Maggie saw that there were more plants throughout the desert landscape. These were sturdy, battle hardened plants. Nothing soft or delicate about them. They were coarse and angular with very few leaves on the branches. The bark on the shrubs was incredibly smooth, as if polished by fine grit sandpaper. From a distance the bark appeared a mundane brown but closer inspection revealed a coppery maroon iridescence, very stunning. Some were tall enough to be considered trees. Though most were bushes. At first glance they looked as if the shrubby trees were dying a very slow death.

"What could survive in such a desolate, inhospitable place?" she thought, but closer inspection revealed much life flowing beneath the hard iridescent bark. These plants were old, but they were also very strong. They looked as though they could withstand any challenge nature threw at them, and already had, unyielding to the harsh extremities of their environment.

The rough, jagged boulders were much larger and no longer in boulder piles. They became more dispersed. The boulders took on very odd shapes, and looked incredibly heavy for their size. None were smooth or round. They were oblong and lopsided, crooked and twisted, uneven and unbalanced, almost as if they were enormous, unfinished chess pieces that had been discarded or rejected long ago by giants. The plants grew around them and underneath them. The plants and rocks were often touching one another. The branches extended towards the boulders and then, once touching, would spire and contort all along the edges of the stone. It was a very intriguing sight. The two were melded in an embrace for survival. In some cases, Maggie couldn't tell where the stone stopped and where the plant took over. It was as if the plants could not survive without the boulders. "How strange?" thought Maggie. Again Maggie's ears popped.

Soon the boulder field gave way to more ascending terrain. Higher they climbed in the little family car. Maggie turned around to see their progress. The view was spectacular. With a cloudless sky, she could see all of the ravines and rolling hills they had passed earlier. She could see the vast, dark green farms of dinosaur kale. On the horizon, she could barely make out a lighter shade of green. The view spread out before her in all directions.

"I can see everything that we have driven across today Dad! Holy smokes!" she proclaimed.

"Wait 'til you see the other side," hinted Father.

"How can any view be more impressive than this?" she questioned. She let out a deep sigh and turned back around to face forward. Again her ears popped. The ground was still flat, and still ascending, but there was no longer any dirt, nor plants, nor boulders. The ground was solid rock, with just a few pebbles scattered about. The rock surface was now smooth, almost polished. "Fun place to skateboard," she thought. Maggie looked farther ahead up into the distance. There it was. Perhaps a mile or more away was the end of the road. Or more accurately, The Great Summit. From this vantage, Maggie could not see it, but she also couldn't see much more ground in front of her. So by default, it had to be a summit. Plus there was a sign at the very top marking something important.

"We should pull off to stretch," suggested Father.

"And eat," chimed Maggie.

"And admire the view," responded Father in stride. He turned off the swamp cooler and rolled down the windows. The air had cooled significantly. No longer an unbearable desert heat, it was comfortable mountain air in the mid 70's. The sensation was very refreshing and rejuvenating. Two days of non stop driving can bore even the most ardent of travelers. Both Maggie and Father were more than ready to use their legs once they had pulled over and come to a stop. Maggie clambered out clumsily onto the hard, stony ground. Her legs wobbled a little from the prolonged lack of inactivity. She hobbled about to get her body back into working order and glanced over to see her father doing the exact same thing.

He glanced over at Maggie and chuckled, "Maybe we should take breaks more often."

"Yeah Dad" Maggie giggled at their current plight.

The two were soon fully operational and began shuffling about. Father opened the trunk and began grabbing various edibles to fashion a makeshift picnic. Maggie decided she better see what was so great about the summit. They had parked about forty yards from the edge. She needed to get a closer inspection. Maggie walked up to the precipice. Maggie noticed that she was having trouble breathing as she headed uphill.

"It's hard to breathe," she shouted to Father.

"You're fine Sweetie, there's less oxygen up here, that's all." he shouted back, stooped over the trunk of the car, rummaging about.

"Wow!" thought Maggie, "I know we were going up in elevation, but I didn't know we were up that high."

In actuality, they had traveled quite high in elevation. Nearly 10,000 feet. As Maggie hiked closer to the edge, the marker sign read clearly, "Great Summit-elevation 10,000 ft." Maggie took no notice but they had, in fact, been traveling on a steady incline for quite some time.

Maggie neared the edge. She still could not see the world below her but she felt its immensity in the pit of her stomach. It made her feel a little uncomfortable. Maggie did not have a fear of heights but she suddenly felt quite unsure about her confidence in walking to the ledge. She thought about turning around. "How can I be so close and still not see anything?" she thought to herself. "Am I on the edge of the world?" Her curiosity was too strong. She had to look over.

She cautiously inched her way to the ledge. Now at eye level with the ridgeline. She inched closer. Suddenly the world below started to come into view. First the horizon came into view, It was surprisingly nonde-script and incredibly far away. The late afternoon sun shone far out across the wide view. The land was brightly lit but showed signs that evening would soon cast everything into darkness. Maggie stepped a lit-tle closer and much of the land in between came into view.

"Holy mackerel!" gasped Maggie.

The land spread out for miles in all directions and the ground below was a long way down. There was too much to see. It was an overload of visual information. Suddenly, Maggie's legs began to buckle. She found herself getting quite dizzy and instinctively kneeled on all fours and looked down at the rock beneath her. She breathed deeply and tried to regain composure but being closer to the ground did not make her feel better. Kneeling with all fours planted on the hard rock, she knew that she was safe, but she could feel the power of the summit next to her. She looked up at the ledge in front of her. Her stomach turned at the thought of creeping closer. She could feel the drop in front of her, as if gravity was pulling her up and over. She had never experienced something so powerful.

She looked back at her father. He was still preparing the meal. She wanted to call him to come and look with her. So she could feel more comfortable, but Maggie was very independent. "I can do this by myself," she said aloud with clenched teeth "I'll just lay on my stomach and look over. I can't fall if I'm already on the ground."

Maggie slid her hands closer to the ledge. A dark, wet palmprint remained where her hand had been.

"My hands are sweating!" thought Maggie. "How are my hands sweating? I didn't even know hands could sweat!"

Maggie wanted to call to her father. "I can do this," said Maggie determinedly with a clenched jaw. She inched her body nervously forward like an awkward caterpillar. Her hands slid uphill on the hard stony ground. She outstretched her arms and straightened her body. She could not feel the drop off, but she knew she was very close.

"One more try," she said with her cheek pressed firmly against the ground. She scooted her legs under her hips, and was now ready for her next wiggle. With arms outstretched, she pushed slowly forward with her legs. Her sweaty palms felt for any change of terrain. There! She could feel the ledge. It was very smooth and rounded. Maggie gripped the ledge and pulled herself to it. She stopped and closed her eyes as she felt her brown, wavy hair begin to dangle. Her face still planted firmly on the stony overlook.

Breathing heavily with her eyes closed tightly, "Ohmygosh… I made it…(breath) I don't want to look… (breath) I have to look."

She lifted her face from the rock and rested her chin on it. She opened her eyes.

Maggie immediately understood why the place was called The Great Summit. The edge of the summit was sheer and vertical throughout its entirety. The summit traveled in a straight line to her left, and to her right, for many miles. It appeared level as well, like a wall made by the same giants who had attempted to build the rock chess pieces. They were much better at building walls than building game pieces. Straight, level and vertical, for thousands of feet, made from one solid mountain of rock.

Maggie lay on the hard rock that constituted the summit. She had no words to describe the immensity of her setting. The land below spread far and wide. Everything below her was small, as if she was watching over a miniature world. She was too high above to see people. She didn't even see any cars. She could barely make out a thin black strip that must have been the highway. The land looked mostly flat, maybe a few hills spread about. She saw a few dark green areas to suggest forests or vegetation but for the most part, the land was brown. Off in the distance, towards the horizon, the land lost its color and texture. It became very monotone, but the late afternoon sun cast a weird light over the landscape which made it hard to discern. She could see water as well.

"The reservoirs," Maggie murmured to herself.

They dotted the land below her. The angle of the sun reflecting off of the water made the reservoirs look black. There were many of them. Perhaps a hundred that she could see. They spanned far out in her field of view.

They snaked in and around what must have been hills. Some were narrow. Others were large and wide. Some were very intricate, spreading out in all directions like arteries pumping from a heart.

Maggie began to feel more comfortable with her lofty vantage point. She let out a sigh of comfort and relaxed her body a little.

"Hungry?" asked Father from out of nowhere.

Maggie turned around startled, "DAD!! Don't just sneak up on me like that! I'm on the edge of a cliff over here!"

Father cracked a smile and chuckled, "I'm sorry Maggie. Are you hungry?" He was holding a woven basket by its handle in his right hand, and a bottle of Sarafornia Bubbly Lava Water in his left hand, Maggie's favorite.

Maggie eased herself away from her perch and cautiously stood up. Once secure, she turned around and looked at her father.

"I am starving!" she replied. She excitedly pranced down to where her father stood. "Where should we eat Dad?" she asked.

Father looked back up at the ridgeline in suggestion.

"No way! I am not eating up there. I will probably vomit just at the thought of it!" retorted Maggie.

"Come on, I know a spot," said Father casually. Without hesitation Father turned away from Maggie and started marching determinedly to their luncheon destination.

Maggie, in disbelief, watched him go for a moment. She had never been abandoned by him before. Although it was only a short distance away, he had always accommodated for her, even the little things. Her stomach growled with impatience, as she followed him. He didn't walk far, just a short distance from the road and onto the summit. He stopped just before he reached the top, kneeled and slid down onto something with just his head protruding above the ridgeline. Maggie saw this and quickened her pace to catch up.

"Are you kidding me?" panted Maggie.

"Pretty neat huh?" said Father nonchalantly.

He was sitting in a carved out section of cliff that had been fashioned into a bench, with just a little space in front to provide wiggle room from the edge.

"How did you ever find this spot?" implored Maggie.

"Oh I used to come here all the time. Many years ago." His tone was just a little hesitant when he spoke. But Maggie hadn't noticed. She was too excited with his discovery.

Maggie plopped down next to her father and immediately gestured towards the basket. "So, what'd you make us?" she inquired.

He reached into the basket and pulled out two freshly made green jello and tuna fish sandwiches.

"Mmmm," said Maggie. She eagerly took the sandwich and ate heartily.

The two ate silently, peacefully perched high atop in their lofty retreat. Maggie looked out at the incredible view before her. Her eyes sparkled against the blue mountain sky. She loved the feeling of being higher than everything else around her, able to watch everything around her unfold. The setting was truly magical. The afternoon sun was losing its bright intensity and was beginning to pick up the first colorful rays of evening. The land was peaceful and quiet.

Out of the quiet, emerged a small breeze. It blew against her wavy brown hair and brushed against her rosy cheeks. It was a slight bit cooler and more brisk than the high mountain air. It felt to Maggie as if it was whispering in her ear. She closed her eyes and listened to the wind. Maggie could understand some of the things it told her. It was from a land she had never been to. Born out of snow covered mountains. It was crisp and clean. It was gentle to Maggie but had an underlying strength. As if need be, it could summon a blizzard in a moment's notice. Maggie had never felt a breeze like this before. She wanted to know about where it was born and what such a place looked like. She opened her eyes and let out a deep breath of satisfaction. She looked at her father fondly.

"I'm having a really good time Dad," said Maggie smiling.

"I am so glad to hear that Sweetie," responded Father. He finished the last of his sandwich and rubbed his hands together to dispatch the crumbs. "Want something to drink?" he asked.

"Ohh yeah!" Maggie loved Sarafornia Lava Water. It was sweet and refreshing, naturally carbonated mineral water that spewed from the volcanoes of Sarafornia. She grabbed the bottle that had been placed at her feet and swigged away.

"Nice spot for a picnic," said Father to himself.

Maggie set the nearly empty bottle down and relaxed against her earthen backrest. "Buuuuurp!" erupted Maggie.

Father turned to Maggie surprised. He looked shocked and humored, "Maggie, excuse yourself." The two chuckled at Maggie's loud outburst. Father reflected fondly of Maggie's mother being able to belch with the same explosive force. "Why I haven't heard a belch that loud since..." he stopped and stared blankly at the hard floor beneath his feet. "Since..." he repeated more quietly and emphatically.

"Since when Dad?" inquired Maggie. She was swaying her feet back and forth, looking at the skyline, still humored by the gas erupting out of her mouth and hadn't noticed his change of heart.

Father did not want bring up any mention of Sarah, if he could help it. Many powerful, memories of her laid locked away, on the route that they would have to take, in order to get to the park. The pain of the past had not healed, even after so many years. He knew that he would have to face some of those memories in front of Maggie, but he was not willing to face every single one that presented itself. He quickly composed himself and got back into character. "Since the Sarafornia volcano last erupted," he said as humorously as he could.

Maggie giggled and smiled sheepishly. She was having a fantastic time. It was easy to forget her troubles when everything around her was so grand and serene. The terrifying experience she had earlier was no longer a clear and present danger. She thought about the destination that loomed far off in the horizon, Yellowsemite.

Maggie felt a tinge of excitement run through her body as she thought about continuing the journey. The thrill of adventure had once again pumped itself into Maggie's blood. She was ready to continue.

"Dad? How do we get down?" said Maggie searching for an exit.

"You ready to get back on the road already?" asked her father surprised in her change of spirit.

"Umm well no. I mean I guess, yeah. It's just that the day's almost over and it looks like we still have a long way to go. I just feel like we should... keep going." She looked up at him hopefully.

Father looked into his daughter's eyes for a moment and took a hesitant breath. It was clear that, despite his underlying struggles, he too was enjoying the time they were spending together. "You're right Maggie," he looked out into the horizon, "We should keep moving."

They both cautiously stood up from their stone fashioned seats, picked up their belongs and headed back to the car. The late afternoon air was noticeably cooling down as they loaded and seated themselves into the vehicle. Father started the engine, engaged into drive and steered back onto the road, towards the the solitary marker sign that read *"Great Summit- elevation 10,000 ft."* and headed closer to the cliff.

After a few moments, "Dad, you never answered my question," said Maggie persistently.

"Ohh," said Father absently as he steered closer to the drop off, "and what question was that Maggie?"

"How do we get down?" stated Maggie with a hint of displeasure. She did not like being in the dark on this matter. As far as she knew there was no way to get down. She had spent a good amount of time earlier inspecting the magnitude of the vertical cliff that she was now driving towards and had seen no road leading down.

"Aww, that question," prompted Father. "Yes I remember." He continued to drive straight to the edge. He was clearly enjoying the event and had no idea that Maggie was quite afraid for her life.

"DAD!" yelled Maggie. "What is your plan for getting down to the bottom?" The car was now nearly at the ledge.

"Oh honey," said Father consolingly, "you need to relax." He pulled up to the marker sign and rolled down his window. There on the wooden post that held the sign, was a small green button. An inconspicuous, downward pointing, arrow had been carved above the green button. Maggie had not walked close enough to the sign to see the small green button. "Feel like taking the elevator Maggie?" said Father casually.

Dumbfounded, "Ummm, I guess so." Maggie had momentarily surrendered any hope of trying to figure out her father's plan.

Father cracked a smile and pressed the green button.

A pleasant female voice reported from the sign, "Going Down".

Maggie's jaw dropped, "You have got to be kidding me."

"Oh no. This is the real deal Maggie," said Father.

In no time at all, a sizable platform emerged silently from the abyssal depths in front of them. It was very flat and modern looking, with sharp, square edges. It had no curb or guard rails. It was as sheer as the cliff that it clung to. It was made completely out of clear, eight inch thick glass. If it weren't for the sky reflecting off its surface, Maggie would not have seen the platform at all. The programed female voice resounded promptly, "Proceed."

Maggies jaw dropped even lower. "You're kidding right? There is no way we are going on that!" she gawked at her father.

He only looked at her in a manner that suggested he had every intention of using the platform.

The two looked at each other in obvious disagreement. At last, "No" said Maggie faintly. He looked at her, expression unchanged. Maggie was not willing to back down, "No Dad. Are you crazy? We are not going on THAT."

Father raised his eyebrows and tilted his head forward as if saying "You can't be serious."

"I am serious Dad" said Maggie in a tone that came out just a little bit scared and whiney.

Realizing that any argument would only worsen the stalemate, Father decided to play his ace, "Do you trust me?"

"What?" she balked.

"Do you trust me?" said Father more firmly.

"Uhh well of course I do bu..." said Maggie

"Well then hold on and enjoy the ride," Father interrupted before Maggie could further plead her case.

He promptly drove the car confidently onto the platform. Maggie squirmed uncomfortably in protest. She wanted to slam the car into reverse. Or grab the steering wheel to turn the car around. But, she could do neither. It was too dangerous. She had to trust her father. She pressed her feet firmly against the floorboard, held on to the sides of her seat cushions tightly and pushed herself as far into her seat as she could. They were now parked completely over the cliff. Maggie had never felt more vulnerable. Her feet tingled with panic at the thought of falling from such a disastrous height. She could once again feel a cold sweat emitting from her palms. She had to relax or she would pass out.

"Dad, if we survive this..." she looked out at the far reaching horizon in front of them, "I'm going to kill you."

"Okay Sweetie," said Father completely relaxed.

The programed female voice prompted, "Please enjoy your descent. Dropping in three. two. one."

Maggie locked herself into her seat tightly, shut her eyes and braced for impact.

"Goodbye," said the female voice.

CHAPTER

7

There was a slight surge in her stomach as the elevator released towards the floor below. Aside from that, there was no other evidence that anything had even occurred. No bumps, no sways or rocking. No wind whirling passed them. The ride was smooth. Perhaps she wasn't going to die after all.

After some hesitation, "Why don't you open your eyes Maggie," suggested Father playfully.

Maggie's curiosity was stronger than her fear. She squinted her left eye just enough to see that her father was looking at her humorously. "What were you so afraid of?" he taunted.

Maggie did not respond. She opened both eyes and looked all around in disbelief. She leaned out against the side window and peered down to look through the clear glass floor. They were definitely traveling down to the rest of the world far below them. Things down there were just a little more discernable. She looked behind her to see the rock wall scroll quickly upward as they fell. It was then that she realized why they did not simply fall to their death. Because of how the platform was secured. There in the wall was a wide slot that had been cut in, running vertically (presumably all the way the bottom). The inside of the slot was shadowed over so she couldn't see what was taking place.

"How the..." gasped Maggie

"They use magnets to control the speed," said Father guessing at Maggie's statement.

"Magnets," repeated Maggie in awe. She did not understand the mechanics, but she was impressed nonetheless. She was amazed at how smooth the ride had been. If it wasn't for all the visual clues, she would have had no idea she was even moving at all.

"Maggie, you might want to turn around. We're almost to the bottom." he advised.

Maggie shot around to see their progress. By the look of things, they were over halfway down. The horizon was no longer flat. Actually, nothing in view was flat. The few hills that were spread about weren't hills at all. They were small mountains. And the land in between them that appeared so flat from above wasn't flat at all. It was hill country. And the hills were dry. They were a golden brown color and looked to be completely covered by dry grass. She could also see the highway much better. It looked to be a very enjoyable road to travel on as it veered in and out of the hills and around the reservoirs.

"Amazing what a change of perspective can do. Wouldn't you say Maggie?" asked father in a leading manner.

Maggie nodded absently. She was too entranced with her surroundings to think about his underlying message. The ground was coming into view very quickly, alarmingly fast. The view was no longer far reaching. They were now level with the tops of the small mountains. Now level with the hills. Maggie was getting nervous, as the platform showed no sign of slowing. If they did not stop soon, they would surely collide with the ground. Maggie looked down. They were going to crash. And then.

"Huhherrrrrrrrr," Maggie groaned as the platform came to a very strong and controlled stop, level with the road. They had landed in a small fenced in area that had several warning signs of stick figures getting crushed by the falling platform. The road picked up right where it left off. There was a gate leading outside of the fenced perimeter. It opened outward by remote. The same automated voice they had left at the top of the cliff could be heard repeating "Proceed."

"Well that was fun," said Father in a relieved tone. "What do you say we keep going until we find a place to stay for the night?"

Maggie was now in complete shell shock. In all her life, she had never experienced so many incredible things in such a short amount of time. She was at a loss for words. She turned to her father and looked at him with a chuckle and a sheepish grin.

"I'll take that as a yes then," said Father turning on his music mix once more. He engaged the car into drive, released the emergency brake, drove off of the level glass platform and onto the road, through the opened gate and out into the land of dry hills and reservoirs.

They drove onward into the evening through the hills. There was just enough daylight remaining for Maggie to make a quick map check. She reached down into the map compartment and sorted through until she found one that read, "Road Map". She pulled it out and gently unfolded it until she could see the general area they were in. She was surprised at how familiar she had become with the map. A week ago, she would not have been able to recognize a single spot. Now, not only could she identify her whereabouts, she could even remember what the places looked like that she had traveled across. Holding the map in her hands, she suddenly realized what a powerful piece of equipment the map was. She was grateful to have learned how to use it.

"What do you see Maggie," asked Father.

"Umm. It looks like we have about 30 miles or so until we get to the first reservoir. Umm. There is a small town there called Lakeport."

"Lakeport?" said Father nostalgically. "Oh boy…"

Maggie looked up at him and waited for a response. He was scratching the 5 o'clock shadow on his chin. He had a lopsided smile on his face and was clearly remembering some fond memory.

"Dad?" interrupted Maggie. "Are we going to stop at Lakeport?'

Father snapped out of his flashback, "Whaa, uhh, no. Out of the question."

"What? Why not? We haven't found anywhere to stay all day," argued Maggie. "There must be a motel we can stay at in Lakeport."

"Oh there is," said Father, "but we are not staying there. Lakeport is a college town. We won't get one minute of sleep in that town. What's the next town?"

Maggie was a little perturbed by her father's response. She looked back down at her map, "Okay… The next town after that is, Reedsport."

Father relaxed his shoulders a little, "Ahh yes, Reedsport. That is much better. We'll stay there for the night."

"Alright Dad but it looks like it is at least an hour away. And it's getting pretty dark out. Are you sure we can't stay at Lakeport?"

"Trust me Maggie. We do not want to stay at Lakeport," said Father firmly. He increased the volume on the stereo and accelerated to cruise speed.

When they arrived at the city limits of Lakeport, the sun had set, the hills had darkened and there was no sign of any reservoir nearby. Lakeport, however; was all lit up and bustling as well. All along the sidewalk young people stirred about. The highway narrowed into a two lane street and cut straight through the downtown area which made for an excellent opportunity to gain a feel for the town.

Several businesses were brightly lit inside and out. They looked very modern and clean. Large ceramic pots grew colorful fountain grasses on the sidewalk in front of the businesses. The streetlights were short, quaint and numerous. Street trees provided a canopy of large, shiny maple like leaves that festooned just above the street lights. Downtown Lakeport made for a very enchanting setting.

As they drove by, Maggie looked into the clean windows of the cafes, restaurants and bars. They were packed with what must have been students who were either learning how to party, or not learning much of anything at all. She could hear loud, excited conversations and the thumping sound of dance music playing in the nightclubs.

Maggie was a little confused, "So this is a college town?" she said skeptically.

Father was clearly enjoying himself watching the frivolity that was occurring outside of the car. "This is Lakeport," said Father confidently.

"So you went to school here?" said Maggie in an inquiring tone.

"Me? No. But uh, your mother. She went to school here.." he murmured, caught a little off guard.

Suddenly, Maggie became much more interested in Lakeport, "What!? Mom went here? Oh you have to tell me about it. You have to tell me everything," Maggie was ecstatic, "Can we stop? Please can we stop? I want to see where Mom went to school. Please Dad. Please!"

"Whoah Maggie. Hang on a minute. Look outside. It's completely dark outside. The campus is closed and all of these cafes are packed. Where are we going to be able to sit down and enjoy ourselves here?" reminded Father.

"I know Dad but I have to see her school. Please," pleaded Maggie. "It means so much to me."

He completely understood her request. She rarely got any information about her mother. He knew that Maggie deserved to know more about her. "Sweetheart. Please. Listen to me. Now is not the right time." He paused to look into Maggie's eyes and choose his words wisely. "How about this? When we return from Yellowsemite, we will come back this way and visit the campus during the daytime. When we can actually see what we are doing. How does that sound? Can we do that please?"

Maggie looked at him the way a victim of a crime might look at her perpetrator. She gave him a good long staredown to let him know that he was not forgiven for being so difficult. She could have cried and thrown a fit. Or screamed and gotten angry. But Maggie was very smart, and independent. She had learned a long time ago that acts of immaturity got her nowhere. She needed to change her approach in order to get what she wanted.

"Okay fine," said Maggie, "then tell me a story about mom right now please." Her mild tone was obviously masking an underlying desire to speak in a manner that was much more harsh.

Father was relieved that the situation had not escalated. He truly did want to show Maggie her mother's college, but he couldn't. He knew that being back on the campus grounds would tear him apart. Even after so many years, he still could not forget the past.

The car continued to progress through Lakeport. Without so much as a warning they had left the more lively downtown section and entered a portion of town was not as brightly lit. The street widened to four lanes and the speed limit increased by 10 mph. This was an area that obviously did not receive the same amount of attention as the part of town they had first entered into. The street lights were dim and the businesses seemed older. This is where the mechanic shops, thrift stores, storage rentals, supermarkets and hardware stores were. The business signs were outdated and the buildings desperately needed a new coat of paint. The lively mood of nearby college life was quickly subdued with the reality of day to day sweat and grease. This section of town was quiet. Inside the car was quiet. The car's engine quietly rolled four tires over the dark gravelly pavement.

"Okay Sweetheart," Father relented at last. He coughed to clear his throat, and his discomfort.

Maggie was no longer interested in being upset. She smiled brightly and settled excitedly into her seat. Seeing Maggie relax made him feel much better about the situation. He cracked a smile and also settled back into his seat.

"Well let's see here. Which one do I tell, aw yes! I've got the perfect story," he reminisced.

Maggie squirmed excitedly.

Father proceeded, "When your mother and I first started dating, she wanted me to drive her up to The Great Summit." He leaned towards Maggie, "You know that cliff we came down a little while ago?" Maggie nodded vigorously, "Well back then, they hadn't built the elevator yet. So from Lakeport, you had to drive 4 hours south of here to where that tall cliff literally crumbles to the ground. Then you have to drive another 4 hours up the summit to reach its highest point. So that's 8 hours each way... And I lived 4 hours away from Lakeport. That's a 24 hour trip. And back then I worked two jobs, six days a week."

"That still sounds so romantic," said Maggie dreamily.

"Yes your mother thought so too. The only problem is that it would take 8 hours just to get to where she wanted to go... And then 8 hours to get back, and I still had to make it to work the next day. To me, She didn't want to go on a date. She wanted to go on a vacation."

"Of course she did," giggled Maggie.

"Of course she did," mocked Father. "Did I also mention that we had just barely met each other? But that was your mother. She knew what she wanted and was prepared to shoot to the moon if that's what it took to get it."

The speed limit increased again by 10 mph. The street lights were now few and far between. If Maggie had taken notice, she would have seen that they were now leaving the college town of Lakeport. But Maggie hadn't noticed. She was fully immersed in the story.

"So you let down Mom?" said Maggie somberly.

"Of course not," retorted Father. "I couldn't just let down your mother... But I also couldn't take her to see The Great Summit either. I worked six days a week in the ferry yard in Shingleton. I would have gotten fired if I even missed one day."

"So what did you do?" asked Maggie.

"Here's what I did. I knew I couldn't risk taking a whole day trip up to the summit so I brought the summit down to us." alluded Father.

"You did what?" Maggie was baffled.

"That's what I did," said Father proudly. "You see, I knew that all your mother really wanted was a nice view to look out at so I blindfolded her and drove her out to one of the taller hills nearby."

"Dad," said Maggie disappointed, "that doesn't sound like a good idea at all."

Father chuckled at Maggie's remark, "Well maybe you're right Maggie but I was between a rock and a hard spot. I had to do something. I couldn't say 'no' to the girl of my dreams."

The street had, once again, turned to highway. The streetlights no longer illuminated . A large sign on the side of the highway read *"Reedsport- 31 mi"*.

"Aw look there Maggie," said Father, "Reedsport 31 miles! We'll be there in no time."

"So did she like it?" asked Maggie. She clearly had no interest in anything that did not pertain to her mother.

"Why yes, as a matter of fact she did," said Father confidently. "You see, before I took off her blindfold, I got out of the car and put a sign post in the ground that read, *'Great Summit- Just for you and me.'"*

"Ah Dad, I didn't know you were such a gentleman," giggled Maggie. She said it jokingly but also could not hide the fact that she was impressed by her father's wit.

Father kept his eyes on the road and smiled, "Well, I fell in love with your mother from the moment I first saw her. I would have done anything for her."

"Except lose your job?" said Maggie in jest.

The car erupted with laughter at Maggie's remark. It felt good to clear the air with laughter. Father was grateful that the situation had not escalated. Talking about Maggie's mother had never been easy for him. It was such a hard thing for anyone to understand. He had never told Maggie what happened to her. It was not something that was easy to hear. He knew that as each day passed, Maggie was growing more and more into a woman. She had every right to know. She needed to know. "But how? How do I tell her?" he thought, "She is old enough, but can she handle the truth?"

"So did you ever end up taking her to the real one?" said Maggie breaking his concentration.

"What Maggie?" asked Father, clearly caught off guard.

"To the actual Great Summit?" explained Maggie.

Father paused to understand Maggie. He closed his eyes and let out a very difficult breath, "Uh, no. No she never got to see The Great Summit." Father grew very somber and still. His cheeks dropped, no longer strong enough to hold a smile. His eyes sagged. He stared at the highway in front of them. He slowed the car down considerably. He still followed the road but was obviously lost deep in thought.

Maggie watched her father. All she could see was his dimly lit face reflecting off of the instrument panel. She had never seen him like this before. He suddenly looked very old and tired, like a pain he had been fighting inside had finally gained strength enough to show itself on his exterior. He looked defeated. Maggie wanted to comfort him. She wanted to change the topic, but also needed to know about her mother. She had grown up with many important, unanswered questions. She knew she was fortunate to have such an amazing role model. He was a good man and a good father. But whenever she wanted to know about Mom she got nowhere. He would crack up or shut down. Maggie had learned to live with unanswered questions. She had learned to live incomplete. She was tired of living incomplete.

"I know she died," said Maggie soberly.

Father said nothing in response. He accelerated the car back up to cruise speed. She had snapped him out of his desperation. He was still uncomfortable, but he was composed. "Maggie," said Father in a consoling tone.

"I know she's dead," repeated Maggie. She folded her arms around herself and turned to stare out at the black night sky outside of her window.

CHAPTER

8

The rest of the way to Reedsport was long and silent. It was very dark outside. No moon illuminated the night. No stars shone bright enough to reveal the rolling hills they were driving through. The only sight was that of black asphalt, two yellow lines lit up by two headlights, and two somber travelers driving through the night.

Maggie did not think. She only stared out into the darkness outside of her window. Father did not speak. He could not face up to the inquiring mind of his daughter. The life he and Maggie's mother had built was a good one. But an accident changed all that. From that moment on, Maggie no longer had a mother. Father no longer had a wife. That woman no longer existed. That was the cold hard truth.

Times like these often cause one to say 'Turn around. I want to go home,' but neither did so. The thought of returning home was always on the table. It was always an option, moreover, the last resort. But neither threw up the white flag. They would reconcile, but not tonight.

Perhaps, that is the ultimate purpose of a road trip. Not to explore the outer world, but to explore the inner world. That which exists in ourselves and our companions. Kept in close contact for long periods of time, things are bound to pop up. Some things will be happy, and some will be sad. So long as the travelers stay true to course, progress will be made. The road will conjure turbulence as will the conversation. So long as the companions seek out their destination, progress will be made.

Eventually, the small settlement of Reedsport emerged. One gas station, a post office, a market and a hotel. There must have been houses nearby but there were no side streets, no front yards or mail boxes that lined the highway. Reedsport seemed more like an outpost than a town. Some barely functional piece of history that had been long abandoned and forgotten. A red neon *'vacancy'* sign led the two to their resting place for the night.

Once again, Father signaled his blinker and slowed down the vehicle on a dark, empty highway. The vehicle became even more gloomy as the tires and engine worked less. The monotonous drone of highway noise had provided a small amount of peace from their subdued unrest. For a brief moment, as the car slowed, all attention was brought back to the previous dispute. For a brief moment, the cramped conditions in the vehicle became unbearable. Neither wanting the company of the other.

The unavoidable silence was quickly substituted for the comforting crunch of tires on gravel. Headlights unveiled a shabby, single story lodge. The rooms stretched out in a straight line before them. The room farthest to the left had a light on outside of its door. A small wooden sign above the door read *'office.'* Father eased the car into a parking spot, turned off the engine and stepped out of the vehicle. Maggie stepped out as well. The two silently stumbled for their belongings, checked into a room and retired for the night.

Maggie awoke well before her father. She must have only slept a couple of hours. The early glow of summer sun was peeking through the heavy drapes of their room. She was restless and needed to move. The pale unadorned walls did not invite activity so she laced up her shoes and decided to venture out and explore the settlement of Reedsport.

She stepped outside of the room, took a mighty stretch, and surveyed her surroundings. The outside air was very enjoyable with no sign of an oppressive heat wave like she had experienced the day prior. A morning breeze blew cool through slightly humid air. She faced the parking lot and highway which flanked around a large, brown rolling hill of dry grass. The sun was still low lying which cast long shadows of the hotel out across the gravel parking lot.

"So where are these reservoirs?" she asked aloud.

"Why, there's one 'round back!" answered an unknown voice excitedly.

Startled, Maggie turned to her left to see a frail old man sitting in a lawn chair a couple doors down from her.

"Excuse me?" said Maggie caught a little off guard.

"You asked where the reservoir was an I told ya. It's 'round back," said the man as straightforward as he could. He leaned back in his folding chair proudly. It made him look very knowledgeable when he did so, like a king presiding over his kingdom, "Might be a little walk to the water though. Been kinda dry lately."

"Oh!" said Maggie. "Thank you," she said, still unsure about the outspoken old man who had interrupted her dialogue. She peered at him briefly to ascertain if he could be a threat, "not at his old age" she thought. She stepped out onto the crunchy gravel and walked briskly around the motel to see what she could see.

The backside descended slowly away and out of sight from the motel. The view was pleasant, nothing magnificent or incredible, just more rolling hills spreading off into the distance. A large hill to her adjacent right made for a bit of a valley before her. She could not see the bottom below due to the curvature of the ground she was standing on.

Still no reservoir though. No water in sight. There was, however; something peculiar about the closest hills facing her. The tops and middle portions of the hills were golden brown and grassy, seemingly normal.

The lower portion had a horizontal delineation traveling at a level progression out and away from view. Below the delineation, the hill was devoid of plant life. Just dark brown earth exposed in the early morning sun.

"Where's the water?" asked Maggie aloud to herself.

"You gotta go down to the bottom ta git to it," replied the old man who had apparently followed Maggie behind the motel.

Maggie instinctively jumped back to distance herself from the stranger. She studied the man to see his ploy. He stooped his frail frame over an old hand made cane. His back was uncomfortably bent forward from what looked like years of hard work. He wore faded denim jeans that were clean but had frayed at the cuffs exposing clean white socks and comfortable looking loafers. He wore a blue and red plaid shirt that looked washed but worn. He held his head low and cocked to one side which looked to be the extent of his ability to do so when standing. He smiled at her fondly with a grin that showed a lot of gum but not many teeth. His eyes sparkled at her excitedly.

Maggie could see that this old man would be no threat to her so she decided to invite his conversation. Something about his bold openness made Maggie feel very comfortable around him. He had been blunt with her so she decided to return the same tone.

"Where's the water?" said Maggie.

"Got used up," said the old man.

"Who used it?" asked Maggie.

"We did," answered the old man.

"I didn't use any of this water," retorted Maggie.

"Oh yes you did," sputtered the old man, "Did you take a bath last night?"

Maggie buckled a little, "Well yeah."

"Do ya have a lawn at where ya live?" asked the man in a patronizing tone.

Maggie squirmed a little, "Of course I do but I don….."

"An how do ya keep that lawn alive?" lectured the old man.

"My dad waters it," Maggie shot back.

"Well where do ya think that water comes from?" pointed the old man. He was no longer smiling at Maggie. He stared at her earnestly, waiting for her to make the connection.

She stared back at him disapprovingly. She had not expected to start her morning with such a turbulent conversation. She thought about the answer before she spoke it. At last she muttered defeatedly, "I don't know, the reservoirs?"

"The reservoirs!" repeated the old man gleefully, "You got it darlin'. If it wasn't fer them reservoirs, ya wouldn't have a pot ta piss in (pardon me bein frank)."

Maggie was clearly caught off guard by the man's blunt honesty. The old man could see that Maggie needed a little more enlightenment to get the big picture so he figured he should explain a little better.

"Okay Darlin, it goes like this. We got this here mountain range to the north of us. The winter storms come in hard and cold. Rain, snow, ice. You drive a couple hours north a here an it can git down right ugly. Any-ways, the snow piles and piles in the winter. When that big yela sun comes back 'round in the spring, it melts all that snow. An seein' how we're downhill of them mountains, all that snowmelt comes down our way. Do ya get my meaning young lady?"

Maggie nodded silently.

"Okay, well a long time ago when folks was movin' 'round explorin tha land an such. A couple a business fellas took a look around and said, 'This here's the place to get our water.' So they built dams. Hundreds of dams to stop the spring runoff and trap it. So's we could use it, fer farmin', fer drinkin, fer everythin. Nowadays, ain't a person on this land that don't depend on these here reservoirs fer somethin."

He paused, took a breath and looked absently at the ground between them. Proceeding with hesitation in his voice, "An it's worked purdy good up until now. Ya see, the last couple a years ain't seen no snow on them mountains. Ain't had no snow melt to fill up these reservoirs. Last couple years, that water level jus keeps droppin' lower and lower." He tightened his leathery lips and licked them. He looked sincerely concerned. Still looking at the ground, "If we don't see a change, ain't gonna be no water for the farms. Ain't gonna be no water for the cities. Ain't gonna be no water in them reservoirs."

Maggie nodded silently. She started to see what the old man was getting at. She looked up and gazed at the modest view before her. She looked at the peculiar lateral cut in the hills across from her. She now understood. "That used to be the water line," she remarked.

The old man lifted his head a little higher to get a sideways view of her. "Yep," he smiled.

Maggie pondered the implications of the information the old man had just given her. She felt a little embarrassed that she had not known where her water came from, or that she was about to run out of it. "Why didn't I know about this before?" asked Maggie, "I never thought about where my water comes from. It's always been there."

"Well, that's the trouble when ya take somethin' fer granted. Don't know how good ya got it 'til it's gone," said the old man in stride.

"So, that's it? If it doesn't snow, we're out of water?" asked Maggie.

The old man moved his cane a little to the side and shifted his weight. He tilted his head up from his crooked neck and looked out at the dry facing hills. "'Fraid so, but we ain't done fer yet. We still got plenty a water in the big reservoirs. They'll last us a while longer." He blinked slowly and looked over to Maggie. He shuffled a little closer to Maggie, as if to tell her something personal and important. He looked at her solemnly, "But ya see darlin, above all else, it comes down to management. If we use the water smart, we ain't gonna run out near as fast. The pipes that carry the water is as old as I am. They leak, need replacin'. The farms usin' the water ain't usin' it smart. I seen a lot of water get wasted away in my day. Farmers gotta make better use a tha water they git. An all them city folk need to know just how important water is, an jus how easy it is to run out. We do that, an we'll be okay."

Maggie looked up into the clear morning sky. She imagined the mountains far out of sight to the north. She imagined them devoid of snow, and the dry land between, devoid of water. For the first time in her life, she wished for a storm, "Why hasn't anyone done anything to fix our problem?"

"As far as this here water shortage is concerned, we's known about it for a while now. Spose them folks runnin' stuff figured it ain't worth worryin' 'bout. Spose they don't want no one findin' out they been reckless with the resources," answered the old man.

"That's not right," protested Maggie. "People have a right to know. They deserve to be informed so they can make smarter decisions with their water."

"Sho do darlin'," said the old man, "'cept these days, ain't nobody wants ta be the bearer of bad news. They's too comfortable livin' in them big fancy houses. 'Fraid they have ta get outside and put in some hard work ta git things right," he paused briefly, "Don't know if you noticed but I ain't no spring chicken. I'm beat up an bent. Had a lot friends end up the same way. We had to use our bodies to build a life. This new generation, don't nobody wanna use they body, jus they brain. They gonna have to use both if they wanna git us outta this mess."

Maggie listened to the old man's wisdom. She now understood the reservoir. She understood the old man. They seemed to be in the same condition. Both had seen better days.

The two fell silent and stared out at the water deprived vista. Maggie closed her eyes and imagined what the view would have looked like at high water. "It would have been very charming," she thought, "Perfect place to have a picnic, and row a canoe." She still wanted to see where the water's edge was, to at least get a perspective on the amount of water remaining.

"So I just walk down this hill to get to the water?" asked Maggie.

"Yep," replied the old man, "It's a little steep goin' down this here curve but eventually it flattens out and meanders around the corner down there. (motioning the course with his skinny, outstretched arm). The water shouldn't be too far around the bend." He looked at her and smiled wide. Despite his lack of teeth, the old man showed a genuine love for life in his smile. His eyes were squinty but sparkled at the notion of adventure. Maggie liked this old man.

She looked out at the quickly rising sun. Father would wake soon. She needed to get a move on if she wanted to be back without causing a commotion. The night before ended on an unhappy note. And with another full day of driving ahead, she did not want to give her father another reason to be prickly and distant. She looked at the rounded slope that disappeared in front of her.

"Just a little ways down?" she murmured.

"Yep," said the old man. "Unless you took a long shower last night," he joked.

Maggie laughed uneasily. Without saying another word, she started walking down the slope. The old man watched excitedly as he leaned against his trusty worn cane.

"Good luck," he said.

Maggie was too focused on walking down the hill to notice the old man's words. She was surprised at how close the old water line had been to the top of the hill. It was easy to find, just out of sight from where she and the old man had chatted. The dry brown grass gave way to the same cut line she had seen on the facing hill. The slope dropped about a foot straight down onto dry mud (which would have normally been under water) and continued to travel down and out of sight. The mud was dark brown and clay like. It had sharp puzzle piece cracks breaking up what would be a uniform texture when moist. She hopped down easily and continued into the lakebed. She found it very odd to be walking on ground that would normally be submerged.

The sun had not yet risen high enough to shine directly into this area. It was cooler down here and quieter. No grass to crunch on. No breeze blew the air. No birds or insects fluttered and foraged about. Maggie was alone down here. The slope steepened and the going became more difficult. Maggie was grateful that the mud had dried into chunks because she was able to wedge her feet into the cracks which served as a natural fashioned ladder. They worked wonderfully to support her weight as she descended lower. "Boy," she thought, "if the mud had dried smooth, I wouldn't be able to get down here. I'm basically scaling my way to the bottom." She stopped and looked about to see her progress.

She had nearly reached the point where the facing hill collided with the hillside she was walking on. It too looked like a steep wall of dried mud. She would be able to walk freely at the junction because the slope did not look nearly as difficult. The seam of the two hills would lead her a little farther down and around the bend, presumably to the water. She turned back to carefully place each foot in the right hold to get down to easier walking conditions. "How deep would I be right now, if the reservoir was full?" she thought, "Could I dive this far down?" She looked back up towards the hotel, "No way! I'm at least 50 feet down."

She reached the juncture of the two hills and walked towards the bend. "I can't believe we've used this much water," she thought, "I have no idea how big this reservoir is but it can't have much water left." She shivered at the thought of running out of water, "Who would let such a thing happen? How would we survive?" Such an uncomfortable thought to think, but if the old man was right, it was completely realistic.

Maggie had reached the bend in the hillside. It curved gradually downward and to the left, just as the old man had said. With steep hillside to her left and to her right, Maggie was now completely surrounded by walls of dried mud. She could no longer see any grassy slopes above. Maggie had to chuckle as she trekked through the narrow ravine. In her wildest dreams, never had she imagined that she would be walking in a realm that was once covered in water.

She was also a little disappointed. She had always imagined the underwater world as a much more interesting place. Where was all the seaweed? And where were the sunken logs and boats? "I feel sorry for the fish," she thought. "Who would want to live in such a boring environment? It's just mud." She was reminded of what she had first read when she researched Yellowsemite on the internet.

"...our country was becoming very bland and boring. Everywhere that people went, it was one city after another, one farm after another, one reservoir after another. The country looked the same wherever one traveled. Quite boring."

"If they only knew how boring it was inside of a reservoir," she thought. "There would have been a lot more people like Johnny Muur." The instant she thought of Johnny, she was flashed back to the terrifying dream that had manifested the day before. Suddenly, Maggie's isolation made her feel very vulnerable. The still, chilly air made her shiver sympathetically. The pliable, hardened mud muted the sound of her footsteps. The steep narrow walls trapped her discomfort and focused it on the unexplainable experience she had with Johnny. The only sound, was that of her apprehensive breath. The only sight, was a brown canvas of earthen wall. She had walked herself into an unavoidable place to repaint the images in her mind.

"It was real," she thought, "I've never experienced something like that before, never." She continued to walk deeper into the ravine and deeper into thought. Were she cognisant of her surroundings, she would have noticed the ground beneath her was softening. Softening from moisture. She probably would have noticed that the dark brown walls also held a faint glow above her, as if reflecting direct morning light. But Maggie was not concerned with such observations. She was locked into her mind, trying to understand the inexplicable. "Why didn't I drown when I was pulled into the water?" she thought. "I was perfectly comfortable. It didn't feel cold. It felt, well, I didn't feel anything, except peaceful." As she continued to walk, the crisp morning breeze she had left behind, had found her once again. She noticed it only indirectly and it made her focus even further on her dream.

"Why was Johnny soaking wet? There wasn't a cloud in the sky. It was sheeting off of him," she thought. "He was excited that I was there, but he acted so strangely. He just stared at me when the eagle dove on me. Why didn't he help me? He didn't even say anything to help me." Maggie stopped walking on the wet muddy ground. "He did talk to me," she said aloud. Her eyes were open wide but she did not see the world outside her. Her mouth was agape, trying to unlock the mystery that confronted her. "He said it twice actually, 'The river gives and the river takes.' Maggie stepped forward to continue walking absently and stepped one foot into shallow water with a "splash". Maggie's concentration was broke. She snapped out of her stupefied internal dialogue.

"Ohh," she said surprised, "I made it to the reservoir." Maggie had absently walked herself all the way to the shore of the receding reservoir.

Her view was quite far and wide. The reservoir must have been a mile across and four miles in length. It was surrounded by very tall rolling hills on all sides. The hills had much of their mass exposed dark brown, just like the dark brown mud Maggie had just walked through.

"Wow, this thing has lost a lot of water," observed Maggie. She stared at the sight before her for a moment, considering all the information the old man had divulged to her. She looked out across the dark, sparkling water. The sun was noticeably higher in the sky.

"Shoot!" she said aloud, "Dad's going to be awake. He's going to kill me!" Maggie immediately turned around to her muddy exit point and sloshed out of the water. She squished her way out of the wet mud and hurried back up the hill to meet up with him. "I shouldn't have been gone so long" she groaned as she clambered up the jigsaw puzzled slope, "he's going to kill me. I just know it," she huffed.

Maggie arrived at the top of the hill in the same condition as she had departed, except she was breathing heavily and her shoes were quite muddy. She paced around quickly to the front of the hotel, crunched across the gravel and fell upon the door to her room. She tried vigorously to unlock the door. It would not open. Maggie had forgotten to take a room key.

"Maybe he hasn't woken up yet?" she thought. She leaned her ear against the door to listen for activity inside.

"Busted," hollered Father humorously from a short distance away.

"Ah HeheHeee," cackled the old man from the same direction.

Maggie turned to face them. She was wide-eyed and had a guilt-strickened look on her face. The two men looked at her jovially. Father was standing next to the old man. He was smiling wide with his arms folded comfortably across his chest. The old man was sitting in his folding chair. He had one arm resting on his worn cane, the other he used to slap against his knee as he laughed uncontrollably.

"Coming back from a stroll Maggie?" presumed Father.

Maggie could tell that her father was not too upset, but she decided to play coy to avoid an underlying reprimand. "Uhh, well I woke up early, I wanted to see the reservoir, but I didn't want to wake you..." Maggie looked at her father earnestly for forgiveness.

"You're lucky this nice man here covered for you." he looked at her sternly and spoke as though divulging an important secret, "I was pretty upset at you when I woke up and couldn't find you" he leaned closer to her speaking quiter and even more firmly, "Don't let it happen again. Okay sweetheart?"

"Yes sir" answered Maggie. She was relieved that he had not lost his composure. It didn't happen very often, but when he did, it was like trying to use an umbrella to stay dry in a hurricane. She did not want to imagine having to continue the drive in a hostile environment. She breathed a sigh of relief and tried to engage with them as best she could.

"Boy I tell ya," laughed the old man. "you shoulda seen the look on yer face."

Maggie smiled shyly at the thought of how she must have looked.

"Bart was just telling me about your little escapade Maggie," said Father.

"Bart? Who's Bart?" asked Maggie.

"Bartholomew Jean Webster," said the old man frankly. "That's my name darlin'. What did ya think it was?"

Maggie felt a little embarrassed that she had not asked for the old man's name earlier. "Bart sounds perfect," said Maggie trying to pacify the situation.

Again the old man chuckled aloud. Maggie chuckled along with him. Not wanting to bring any more attention to her (apparently unabashed) behavior. "Yeah, the reservoir is really low Dad," said Maggie focusing the topic elsewhere, "It's kind of disappointing."

"It is Maggie," responded Father. "We are really going to be in trouble if we don't get some snowfall this coming winter."

"Yep," affirmed the old man, "That'd be three years, back to back without so much as a drop in the bucket."

Maggie sighed and looked out longingly across the highway to the dry hill on the other side. Suddenly, her empty stomach growled loudly. Both men heard it as well.

"Woah Maggie," exclaimed Father. "We better get some food in you. Stay right here. I'll go get you some pumpkin muffins." He turned and walked to the car.

"Dad, they're inside the room remember? We brought them in last night," reminded Maggie.

"Sweetie, the car is already loaded and ready to go," informed Father. "What did you think? That I was just going to lay in bed all morning?" He walked to the trunk of the car and began shuffling things about in search of the muffins.

Maggie and the old man watched her father collect a meal. "He musta woke up a couple minutes after you disappeared down that holler," chimed the old man. "He was a little worried that you disappeared on 'im. I set 'im straight though. He didn't git up in arms or nothin. Set right about ta gettin' all packed up. He must trust you young lady. That's mighty special. Don't never do nothin' to lose that trust."

Maggie leaned to listen to Bart but said nothing. She just watched her father fondly. She was so grateful that the morning was off to a good start, especially since the night before had ended so poorly.

The old man watched Maggie. He studied her, "There's somethin' special about this young lady." He thought to himself, "Reminds me of somebody…" He looked at her while he tried to recall the figure in his memory. "Ahh," he said at last, "I know I knew'd it!"

Maggie looked over at the old man inquisitively. "Knew what?"

He licked his lips as if preparing to say something very important. He was no longer smiling. He leaned back against his faded folding chair and took on a lordly impression. His dark sparkling eyes, focused straight ahead, deep in concentration. Maggie watched inquisitively. At last the old man cleared his throat and spoke in a most dignified voice, *"I fell upon this land by chance, as my home balanced on the precipice of life and death, pushed by the wrought and sprawling woes of mindless expansion. Dare I dreamt that this bounty that lay before me existed unspoiled. That its fruits were solely of the earth, water and air. The hands of man had not touched this land. It was cleansed pure by its own accord. Though never before had I experienced such raw nature, never before had I felt more human. Into her bowels I explored and found only more uninhibited grandeur. This gift that was placed upon me, I place upon you. Dare not change this land for better or worse. Instead only take audience and watch its processions unfold before you. That is the gift. I know now why the wild heart beats. I know why the wild heart beats."*

Maggie's jaw dropped, stunned by the old man's testimony. The old man gathered himself and smiled humbly at Maggie.

"I know that quote," said Maggie at last. "Those are the opening lines of *A Special Land*."

The old man nodded assertively, "Yep, those are the lines he used ta convince the gobna and preseedent they oughta make a park outta Yellersemite," he paused. "I know'd you was special when I seen ya. I know'd you had one," said the old man confidently.

"Had what?" asked Maggie innocently.

The old man looked at her as if the the answer was obvious. "A wild heart," he said bluntly.

Father's footsteps crunched across the gravel parking lot to deliver a package to Maggie's growling stomach. Maggie stared at the old man in disbelief. The old man had read her like a weak poker hand. Maggie was astounded and speechless. Though she did not understand the old man, apparently, the old man knew her better than she knew herself. She barely noticed when her father handed her a moist pumpkin muffin.

A faint, "Thanks," was all she could muster. The three faced each other without talking. Each person waiting for the other to speak.

"Umm, are you ready to go Maggie?" Father said at last.

Maggie stared at the old man, like a deer caught in the headlights of an oncoming vehicle, "Umm, sure Dad. Whatever you say."

"Nice chatting with you Bart" said Father. He turned and crunched back to the car.

Maggie did not have a word to say. She absently followed her father across the driveway to the car. Father had already started the vehicle and was seated, ready to go. Maggie reached the car, opened the door and looked back at the old man. He just stared back at her like an excited spectator in a crowd. She turned back to the car and slipped down into her seat. Just as she was closing the door, she heard the faint words of the old man over the idling engine, "The river gi…."

CHAPTER

9

"SLAM!" Went the door. Maggie swung around to try to see the old man finish what he was saying. Although she could no longer hear him, she might be able to read his lips. But he had already finished. He just stared back at the car. Father engaged the car into drive and started moving.

Maggie was beside herself. She looked to her father, to see if he had picked up what the old man had said. He showed no reaction. He was focused on entering the highway.

"Did you hear him?" asked Maggie uncomfortably.

"Hear what?" asked father.

"He said something about the river," Maggie looked quite concerned and nervous.

"Umm, No. He mentioned a lot about the reservoir. I don't recall anything about a river."

"No Dad," interjected Maggie. "Just now! He said 'The river gives,' Johnny Muur told me that yesterday, err, I mean he dreamt those words, argh, I dreamt those words." Maggie looked quite uncomfortable.

Seeing Maggie so distraught made him quite concerned, "Sweetheart, do you want me to turn around? We can go ask him what he said if you'd like."

"No...no Dad. I'm fine... I'm fine," Maggie's stiff shoulders and arched back indicated otherwise to her father.

"You sure?" he asked leadingly, "It's no trouble to backpedal a little, especially if it will make you feel better."

Maggie finally sat back into her seat. She crossed her arms tightly and began biting at a thumbnail. She stared, fixated at the glovebox in front of her.

"Maggie? Do you want me to turn around?" said Father very deliberately.

"No Dad, it's okay... I'll be fine," her tone had calmed and she appeared a little more composed, though she was still far from normal. "She'll get over it," he thought to himself. He shrugged his shoulders and accelerated onto the highway.

Maggie was in no mood for talking. She had just been blindsided by an old man who, somehow, knew about her dream. "Did he really know?" She thought, "How could he know? It's not possible. Maybe he said something similar and I just heard him wrong." Maggie knew that was not the case. Even over the sound of the running engine, she had heard him clearly. He had repeated the same ominous words that Johnny had said, two times, during her haunting dream.

"How is that even possible and why would he say something like that?" she pondered. It chilled Maggie to the bone to consider the implications. "Does he know something bad is about to happen to me? Why wouldn't he just say so?" She felt very violated that the old man had said something so personal to her, and just out of the blue, as if it was no big deal. "It's a very big deal!" thought Maggie. "What the heck is going on?"

Outside of Maggie's internal conflict, the world was peaceful and pleasant. The view had cleared off to the right to expose the western shore of Reedsport Reservoir. Maggie had discovered it earlier in the morning after trudging through the dried mud ravine behind the motel. An expansive blue skyline cast itself in front of the travelers. There would be no mountain ranges to cross today. Only hills and reservoirs, and perhaps if their pace sustained, The Flat Grey Dirt Desert.

None of these observations concerned Maggie. She was fixated on understanding the relevance of that frightening phrase. "What does that even mean?" she thought defensively. "Maybe this is just common knowledge. Maybe Dad knows."

"Dad?" asked Maggie.

"Yes Sweetie?" answered Father.

"Have you ever heard the phrase: 'The river gives, the river takes'? Is it like a song or something?"

"Can't say that I have Maggie... I suppose it might make for a catchy song though." He then began composing a melody for the potential song, "The river gives, ba duhn ta duhn, the river takes, wah wunt wa wah."

"Ugh, nevermind," said Maggie somewhat annoyed at her father for making light of her question. "Maggie," she thought to herself, "you're just going to have to figure this out on your own." She scratched her scalp contemplating "What if Johnny wrote that phrase in his book?" she thought. I haven't finished it yet, maybe it's in there. That would be nice." At last Maggie exhaled a breath of relief. She reached into the glove box and pulled out her copy of A Special Land. Holding the book in her hands made her a little nervous. The last time she held it, she was nearly drowned by an enormous, invisible eagle.

"Dad?" Maggie laughed uneasily.

"Yes Maggie?" answered Father.

Somewhat hesitantly Maggie replied, "I'm going to read, but if you see me start to fall asleep, will you please wake me up?" She tried to give her father a lighthearted smile but all that came out was an awkward grimace.

Father could see she was truly concerned. He, however; was not, but he didn't want to give the notion that he thought Maggie was grossly over-reacting and superstitious. "Sure thing Sweetie," he said reassuringly.

Maggie tried to find the place where she had left off but she really didn't remember. "Where was I? Where was I?" interrogating herself, "umm, where did my dream start? Uhh the wooly mammoths and the lily tree grove? Now is that actually in the book or did I dream that too?" She quickly skipped to the last folded page corner she had bent as a book-mark. She searched for a beacon of memory. The only thing that was rec-ognizable was the musky scent of aged paper wafting into her nostrils as she flipped through the pages.

"Err!" she growled, "Dad? I'm not saying this because I'm bored but how much longer 'til we get there?"

"Let's see here. Well we should be able to get to the desert by evening, and if conditions are good, we should get to the park by tomorrow after-noon," Father said optimistically.

"Okay good," said Maggie in a very serious tone, "I have to reread this book, from the beginning."

"Okay?" said Father skeptically. "If you say so... so much for a travel buddy."

Maggie did not want to spend the entire day reading, but her concern was too great. Too many unexplainable events had occurred for her to pass everything off as coincidence. She needed to find an answer, and the only applicable resource she had was the book.

"I'm sorry dad," said Maggie solemnly. "Please wake me up if you see me sleeping."

"10-4," said Father plainly.

Maggie settled into her seat and began reading. It was strange that even though she had read the beginning before, it was as if she was reading it for the first time. Different things stuck out in her mind than before. She also found more meaning in the scripture. Johnny's thoughts had become more personal to her. She looked for meaning in everything that she read, as if she had given life to the tattered old book.

She sat for several hours, reading incessantly, as Father drove them through the hills and along the receding banks of the reservoirs. He stopped for gas. Maggie took no notice. He played his music. Maggie sat, eyes fixed down at her book. At one point a large snapping turtle crossed the road on a blind curve. Father had to swerve swiftly to avoid colliding with the lethargic creature. Maggie didn't even bat an eye at the ordeal. She was on a mission.

By midday, both were starving and needed a good stretch of the legs. Father parked at a reststop that sat atop one of the higher hills which over-looked one of the larger reservoirs, aptly named, Big Reservoir. The outside air was placid, just a bit warm and balmy. An intermittent breeze blew the herbaceous scent of dry grass and the abundantly pungent essence of mud. Below them, Big Reservoir had plenty of freshly exposed mud around it's gradually sloped shoreline. Even despite the strong odors, the scene was very pleasant. Big Reservoir's immensity spanned out below them. It had several lush, low lying islands scattered about. The islands were all about the same height (just a few feet above the waterline) and were a brilliant shade of green. She could hear the distinct, but indistinguishable sound of insects chirping and foraging, scattered in and amongst the dried grass around her. She could also hear the hiss and clank of the car's engine, as its metal components contracted and cooled, no longer being fired by combustion. Maggie walked around to the trunk of the vehicle with her father. The two began to forage around for sustenance.

"Any luck yet?" asked Father as he pulled out a bag of Cousin Lefty's ginger and olive flavored ferret jerky.

Maggie pulled out a jar of salted sun-dried mealworms. She opened the jar and stared longingly at its contents. "No, not yet. I mean I'm finding lots of good stuff. But not what I'm looking for," she sighed.

He gazed back at Maggie. She was still clearly distraught. Maggie had always been attentive when it came to reading, but he had never seen her so feverish about a topic before. He wanted to help. But how? He had no idea what Maggie was dealing with. After all, it was just some silly dream. He scruffled her wavy brown hair and walked to a nearby picnic table. Maggie grabbed her mealworms, a gallon of water, and joined him. The two sat together without talking. The only noise they made was with their teeth chewing on crunchy bugs. They looked out at the view in front of them.

It was another beautiful day. The sky was very clear. No dust or pollution discolored the sky. The air was clean. Far off ahead in the distance, an orange speck emerged over the horizon. The speck stayed relatively unchanged for some time. It slowly started to grow in size. Maggie became momentarily distracted by the speck. The mass continued to grow.

"What is that?" said Maggie somewhat intrigued.

"I'm not sure," said Father as he shielded his eyes to better see. "It's not a jet. Birds? Could be birds."

Maggie had never seen birds from so far away before. Except for the eagle! Maggie's hair stood up at the notion. "They don't have orange eagles do they Dad?" asked Maggie alarmed.

Father chuckled, "I don't think so."

"You don't think? Or you don't know?" she urged.

Father turned to Maggie who was poised to have another breakdown, "Maggie, relax. There are no orange eagles. At least not around here."

Maggie was not convinced. They watched the orange mass continue to slowly grow in size as it travelled towards them. The aggregation only got larger and larger. It looked like an endless airborne river of orange flowing towards them. After a while, they could see the distinct flapping of wings emerge in the hoard of orange. There had to be thousands-correction-tens of thousands of them. They weren't birds though. The wing beats of birds are graceful and delicate. These were not so, they were more deliberate and angular, almost mechanical. These were large as well, their wingbeats were much slower than that of a bird. Suggesting that either their bodies were much lighter or wings were much larger.

"What are they?" gawked Maggie. She no longer felt threatened. This flock of unidentified flying creatures posed no immediate threat. They were, however; drifting in her direction, at a slow and exertive pace. The drove of orange grew larger and more definitive. Such a strikingly beautiful sight, this bright band of tangerine set against the clear blue sky. The onlookers were bedazzled. The flock silently flighted closer and closer.

"Ahhhhhh," Father said at last, "I know what they are."

"What?" implored Maggie. "What are they?"

"That is a flock of sovereign butterflies," divulged Father.

"Wow!" delighted Maggie.

"They're often a prelude to bad weather," informed Father. "You can probably guess that they don't fair well in wet or windy conditions. They only leave an area when there's a chance that their wings might get beat up."

Maggie listened intently without responding. She could now make out some of the individuals in the front of the pack. Their wings were a pure bright orange, their bodies hung like long black pendants.

"They're coming right this way!" exclaimed Maggie.

"It certainly appears so," reveled Father.

From the vantage of the rest stop, Maggie and her father had a pristine view of the procession since the butterflies were flying more or less level with the hilltop. The enormous squadron fluttered peacefully around the spectators. The butterflies slowly, and determinedly, made their way down towards Big Reservoir.

The butterflies were quite large. Their bodies were the size of Maggie's forearm with wings the size of sewer covers. They flapped their way around the rest stop and began to descend upon the reservoir.

"I don't believe it," gasped Maggie.

The butterflies fluttered down to the water, more specifically, the islands. Or were they islands at all? Maggie was surprised to see the butterflies land in a vertical position, with their head and long antennae pointed skyward once they had landed.

"Those aren't islands at all, they're reed beds. That explains why they are all the same height and color," discovered Maggie. One by one the butterflies dropped onto the reed beds. The procession took several minutes to complete.

Maggie and her father were completely enchanted by the scene. What a joy it was to watch the benevolent creatures haphazardly search for a landing space on an already crowded reed bed. The bucolic green "islands" were soon engulfed by radiant orange. Still, more butterflies flew around the hill and descended to their resting place. These individuals were the last to show up. They were the 'Old Timers' and 'Graybeards' of the flock. Their efforts to stay aloft looked a little more strained. They were the ones who had not escaped previous foul weather events unscathed. Tattered wings, and wing tips were worn and frayed. Some even had holes through the wing, which were most likely caused by hail or heavy raindrops. Still they flew with the same determination as the younger, faster crowd leading the pack. Before long, even they managed to find a place to rest. And all the commotion was over.

The islands of butterflies sat as motionless as the reeds. Maggie considered that if she and her father had shown up at this moment, they would have not known what the orange islands were.
"Strange," she said aloud.

Father said nothing in response. He reached in his bag and pulled out another piece of ferret jerky. He brought the piece to his mouth and ripped off a chewable chunk with his molars. He chewed vigorously and stared out at the butterfly mass, mesmerized.

The two watched the butterflies from their vantage point for a short while longer, but soon enough they were back in the car, and on the interstate. Father whistled away to his musical medley, and Maggie buried deep into her book. The moment she clasped her seatbelt she was back onto the task at hand. Deep into the adventures of Johnny in the wilderness she traveled. Every page or so she would intentionally stop reading and pinch herself to make sure that she had not drifted to sleep.

Then back into the book she would dive. Being chased by honey badgers and swimming with river otters. Tracking beaver with Ahwahnchee hunters, diving for freshwater lobsters beneath mountain waterfalls. She read about all of these amazing things but still could not find mention of her fortuitous phrase.

Midday progressed into afternoon. Maggie was having trouble reading. Her neck and forearms were extremely uncomfortable and sore from being held in various reading positions. She wanted to stop, but she had to find something that would help her understand that mysterious, powerful phrase. She strained against the urge to stop reading.

"Keep going Maggie," she said firmly to herself.

Father jumped in his seat. Maggie hadn't so much as moved in the last hour. He had given up on having a travel companion. Maggie took no notice as she continued reading.

The remainder of the book was Johnny's closing arguments on why Yellowsemite should be a National Park. His final thoughts before he disappeared, presumably, back into the wilds of Yellowsemite, never to be heard from again. Maggie puffed her cheeks in anxiousness. She looked down at the pages below her and continued reading.

"Please be here," she thought to herself.

"... My heart is filled with gratitude in the knowledge that such a wild land exists. It is imperative that such a place be deemed as sacred, and securely absorbed within the foundation of this glorious nation. The obvious physical beauty as well as the great mysteries bound here hold innumerable benefits to society.

Here is a playground for the young and the old. Here is a school for those who wish to learn of the wonders of the wild world. Here is a canvas upon which an artist will unveil a masterpiece. Here is the place where explorers will find their treasure.

The many mysteries of nature are illuminated in this pristine pocket of wilderness. Watching these grand processions play out in this open amphitheater will humble your anxious soul. This land will cleanse corrupt thoughts into images of delight, awe and wonder. This is a land of salvation.

Salvation indeed for as it hurts this weary heart to speak frank I must admit the shameful truth that clouds over the legacy of mankind. We have sought to build a future that excludes all other life from prosperity, often selfishly, ravenously. As though we are the reason the world is wide and wondrous. When in fact we are wide and wondrous because of the world. And as tall as towers may rise, they pale at the grandeur of a mountain sunrise.

Friends,

We are out of control. It exudes itself like sweat from a furrowed brow. For in the pursuit of a better life, we have garnered no more stability than when our ancestors first set out from modest beginnings. Yes, survival is easier. And many of us now live to an old age. But our composure is paper thin and fleeting. Feuds persist throughout generations. Expansion trumps progress, and the world is buttressed and burdened by the selfish pursuits we deem necessary. Harmony is humorous. Peace is piecemealed and parceled away. And every night, we try to fall asleep, silencing the voice that tells us we have been doing it all wrong.

Let not the elegance of nature fall to the wayside. Instead allow us to be humbled by that which we cannot create, nor replicate. Let this place be a source of gratitude to the magnitude of life. Let our children, and their children's children, see a land unchanged by the biased beckoning of a belligerent humanity.

And perhaps, by doing so, the true greatness of humanity shall reveal itself.

I do not expect that all will love this land as I have grown to love it. I do not expect every child to wish to visit this land of wonder. I do expect all to understand the requirement to secure some places to their own natural processes. I do expect all to realize that the hand of man is not always necessary for the betterment of the world. For these truths are made self evident in the wilds of Yellowsemite. And this realm shall forever bear testament to the ideal that some places should remain forever wild.

I must now go back to the earthly heaven that exposed itself to me five years ago. For I am incomplete without it. A hollow vessel that can only be filled with clear, running water, unobstructed starlit nights and green leaves that pat against themselves in a fresh breeze. I go now to seek out Yellowsemite's greatest treasure, the emerald trout. A mystery that has eluded me throughout my exploits, save for that very first day whence I stumbled upon its sapphire realm. The river gave me a gift that day, but it also took something from me in return.

I am an empty vessel. I pray that the river will give me that which I yearn for. One can only speculate as to what it will take as compensation. For the river gives and the river takes. That is its way.

Go to the mountains I say

To the verdant valleys in between

Let a silent sky with starlit hue

Breathe some life inside of you

Swim the rivers

and drink the waters

For these are a virgin nature's

daughters

Go to the mountains I say

and springtime meadows at your feet

Blaze a glory undescribed

nourish a soul revived

Ancient beast may roam free

and thrive

I'm going home

And glad to be alive

Go to the mountains I say

Feel the river sway

Let the children play

On this righteous day

Sincerely,
J. Muur.

CHAPTER

10

Maggie closed the book. The static noise of the highway returned to her hearing. She looked blankly at her faded denim jeans and at the floorboard at her feet. She had found what she was searching for, and so much more. Father had not noticed. He hummed a familiar tune absently to himself. Maggie contemplated her discovery.

"What an absurd thing to say… What was taken from him?" she thought.

She exhaled deeply and sat back in her seat. She looked longingly out of her window into the world outside. It was now late afternoon. The land had changed. There were no longer any hills or reservoirs in front of her, only an oily, black highway laid upon a flat landscape of somber grey. Maggie looked behind her to see the boundary of hill country, quite a ways out in the distance. The hills stretched out to the left and right for miles. To Maggie, the smooth, golden slopes tucked into the flat, grey landscape like bare feet digging into a soft carpet.

"Don't tell me you're finished," exclaimed Father.

This time Maggie was the one who jumped. "I uhh…. (clearing her throat) Yes! I finished," blurted Maggie.

"Everything turn out the way it was supposed to?" inquired Father.

"Ummm, yeah. I guess... I found what I was looking for," said Maggie a little reluctantly.

"That's great!" said Father. "Now we can lay the issue to rest," assumed father.

Maggie hesitated before she responded. She looked at Father. He did not appear to be concerned in the least. "He must think I'm crazy," she thought. "Sure Dad," said Maggie solemnly. The car fell silent for a brief moment.

"Notice anything different?" asked Father leadingly.

Maggie looked at him somewhat sarcastically and fixed her gaze on him until he glanced back at her. "Let's see here," said Maggie in a smart aleck tone. "Well, I don't see anymore hills...hmm... or reservoirs...but we're in a place that's flat...hmm..that has grey dirt, and looks like a desert. Hmm, I wonder where we could be?"

Father chuckled at her chiding remark. He was glad to see that Maggie's wit had not suffered even though she had been noticeably distraught ever since departing from Reedsport. He resettled his gaze on the road ahead. Unbeknownst to Maggie, he too had felt an overwhelming uneasiness ever since he had taken Maggie to The Great Summit. Memories of the past started trickling into his mind. Memories that he had worked so hard to keep locked away.

Suddenly, something bounced against the driver's side window and disappeared out of view.

Maggie noticed it out of the corner of her eye. "What was that?" she asked curiously.

"I have no idea," replied Father. "It came out of nowhere. Whatever it was, it wasn't very harmful. I don't think it even left a mark. There!" he pointed. "In the road ahead."

Maggie jolted forward and strained against the dashboard. She looked just in time to see an odd white orb the size of a basketball, amble awkwardly off of the road and back out in the grey desert. The object didn't bounce like a basketball, however; it kind of hobbled and rolled in an unbalanced fashion, almost like a drifting tumbleweed.

"What is that?" asked Maggie somewhat perturbed.

Father knew what it was. He had heard stories about them from family members. "What does it look like?" he asked rhetorically, "It's a cotton ball."

Maggie watched the ball drift out of view as the car drove past. "Oh!" she remarked, turning her attention back to the road ahead, "That's what they look like. I remember you telling me about them when I was a little girl. I never thought I'd get to actually see one."

"Well now you have," replied Father flatly. "Oh look, here come some more."

A small cluster of cotton balls rambled across the road a ways ahead of them. Maggie found the sight to be quite humorous. "They look harmless to me. Why do I remember them being a problem?" she asked. Another cotton ball hit the car. This time it bounced off the hood.

Father was focused on driving. Without turning his attention to Maggie he answered, "Well, if you recall the story. It was Grandpa Max who got into trouble with them. His situation was a little bit different. He got stuck driving in a cotton ball storm. I think there were a lot more than what we're dealing with."

"Oh..." replied Maggie still focused on remembering the story. Several more cotton balls bounced across the road. The two companions drove on through the desert in silence, watching the progression of drifting cotton balls. They appeared to be gradually increasing in numbers.

"I wonder…might be…storm," mumbled Father to himself.

Maggie overheard some of the conversation but couldn't make everything out. "What was that Dad?" she asked.

"Huh?" he asked. "Ohh, I was just noticing that there seems to be a lot more of these things… I'd hate for us to get stuck in a storm of them." He drifted back into his thoughts.

Maggie looked at him in contemplation. "Yeah," she said at last. "Me too."

They drove on through the cotton balls. Maggie watched them closely. They continued to grow in concentration. She looked out passed her father to see them tumble towards the car. They were scattered all around her field of view. All bouncing steadily in the same direction across the road. Maggie was beginning to get a little concerned.

"Dad?" asked Maggie.

"Yes Sweetie?" replied Father

"I feel like Grandpa Max did not have a good experience with cotton balls… I feel like you warned me not to get stuck in a storm of them," she admitted.

Father grumbled a little before answering, "I remember the story too Maggie. We're not in a storm of them." He looked to the side to assess the status of the cotton balls, "This is more like a flurry, yeah, definitely a flurry. Not a storm."

Maggie raised her eyebrows skeptically in response. She was not convinced by his assessment. "Alright," she replied dubiously.

It wasn't long before the flurry intensified into something more like a storm. "How about now Dad? Is this still a flurry to you?" she asked apprehensively.

Father rubbed his forehead with his thumb and answered in submission, "Umm, yes. This is more stormlike to me."

Trying not to sound nervous, "So what do we do then?" asked Maggie

"Drive steady and stay in your lane," he quickly reported back.

She could hear the stress in his tone. He was concentrating. "Probably best to keep questions to a minimum," she thought. She did not agree with her father's logic though, "What if there's an accident in front of us? How will we see it with time to stop?" She shifted in her seat uneasily and started to bite at her thumbnail.

Father knew what that meant. "She's is thinking too much," he thought. "We're going to be fine sweetie. These things aren't too much trouble when they come from the side. They just kind of bounce off the car. One might get stuck on the outside mirror but that's about it. It's when they come straight at you, that's when it gets a little more tricky," said Father consolingly.

She glared at him, "Well then why do I remember you saying that we shouldn't drive in them?"

Her father relaxed a little, "Ahh, Grandpa Max was in a convertible. And the cotton weeds were coming directly at him. Yeah, when they're thick like this, you don't want them coming straight at you. It can definitely get more difficult. And in Grandpa Max's case, it was even worse. He couldn't get his convertible to close its canopy so his cab got filled with cotton weeds. In the end, it worked out okay. He ended up using that very cotton to sew some new shirts."

"Is that why he always smelled so funny?" asked Maggie.

"Sort of," answered Father.

He had calmed her enough to ease her apprehension, a little. "Yes, we'll be fine as long as the wind doesn't shift," she said, looking out the window. She watched the basketball sized cotton weeds bounce in procession across the road. There were hundreds of them.

"But what if the road turns into the wind?" Maggie, once again, began to ponder herself into slight panic. "Don't do it, don't do it," she thought. She wanted to grab the GPS in her backpack to see what was ahead. "I'm just worrying too much," she thought. "We're on the flattest place I've ever seen. Why would we need to turn? Don't be ridiculous," she told herself.

The car swerved a little. "What was that?" Maggie quickly asked.

"Nothing dear, the breeze picked up a little. That's all," answered Father.

"That was more than a breeze Dad," retorted Maggie. The car swerved again, but this time it also leaned for a brief moment before returning to its normal course. Maggie stirred restlessly, "Umm".

"I know, I know Maggie. It's getting stronger," Father interrupted.

The cotton balls were now whipping across the road. Maggie could actually hear the faint "ponk..ponk.ponk......ponk ponk ponk" of the cottonweeds bouncing off of the side of the car. There were so many cotton weeds she could barely see the car in front of them.

"Okay Maggie, you win. Look on your GPS and find the next pull out. I guess we're going to have to wait this one out," said her Father relenting.

Maggie quickly pulled it from the outer side pocket of the backpack at her feet. Again the car swerved in the wind. It seemed like an eternity waiting for the GPS to catch a signal. Finally, her location came up. Without hesitation, she went straight to search mode for *"rest stop"*. The screen listed *"1 result found- 5 miles"*.

"Rest stop in 5 miles Dad," reported Maggie.

"Good, in front of us?" Again the car swerved heavy to the right.

"Umm," she looked at the screen. "Ohh no!" Maggie gasped.

"What is it?" He asked.

Maggie didn't answer. She just stared at the screen. Turning alertly to his daughter, "Maggie, what do you mean 'oh no?'" demanded Father.

Maggie looked up from her screen, out in front. She glanced to her left and then back down to the screen. "Dad, the road turns up ahead. It's going to point us straight into the wind," said Maggie defeatedly.

Father looked at her for a moment and then relaxed back in his seat. He let out a deep breathe and returned his full concentration to the road. "Five miles to the rest stop?" he asked determinedly.

Maggie looked up from her GPS screen and stared out in front of her. She dropped her shoulders defeatedly. "Yeah Dad," she sighed, "five miles".

The cab of the car fell silent as the deluge of cotton balls bombarded the exterior. Two occupants fixed their attention only on the eminent threat ahead. Through the bouncing polka dots of cotton, the road began to slowly turn into the wind.

As the car followed the road into the wind everything began to go white. The cotton balls were so numerous that they blanketed nearly all the field of view. Father leaned forward into the windshield to try and see into the canvas of cotton. Maggie did the same. Only brief patches of black highway became exposed, and only for an instant at a time.

"Dad," strained Maggie, "I don't think we can drive in this..."

Father's focus was locked solely on the highway. "I know Maggie," was all he could muster.

The car slowed significantly. The inside of the car became uncomfortably quiet. Maggie and father engaged their total attention straight ahead, desperately seeking clarity of what lay in front of them. Outside the cotton ball storm blasted relentlessly upon the windshield. The small vehicle shook ferociously from an unrelenting headwind.

"What can we do Dad?" pleaded Maggie. "We can't stop. What if another car rear ends us? And what if a car in front of us is stopped?"

Maggie tried not to break her father's concentration but she could not help but squirm restlessly in her seat. She grasped the seat cushions on each side of her. Her grip slipped as her palms sweated involuntarily. Each second passed, with as much longevity as an ice age. Maggie clenched her tongue between her jaws in an attempt to alleviate the stress.

"Brrrrrrrrrrrrrrrrrrrrrrrrrrrrrrrrrrrrrrr!" shook the car as it drove over the rumble strip.

"Dad!!" shrieked Maggie.

"That was just the rumble strip Maggie," said Father as soothingly as he could. "That's what it's there for. We just drifted too far to the right, that's all."

"Brupbrupbrupbrupbrupbrup!" retorted the car.

"Then what was that?" pleaded Maggie. She was becoming hysterical.

"Umm those were the reflectors of the passing lane. We, uhh, drifted too far left." His tone took that of a person who was finally admitting guilt.

"Dad!" said Maggie scoldingly.

"Not now Maggie!" bellowed Father. He was now done with trying to pacify his daughter's discomfort.

Maggie jolted back into her seat. She exhaled loudly and stared unblinking at, what she presumed was, the road in front of her. For the first time on this adventure, Maggie considered the possibility that she may not actually get to visit Yellowsemite. She became very sad at the thought. "I don't want to give up," she thought to herself. She sighed and looked at her reflection in the side view mirror. She needed a bath.

She saw a yellow flash briefly ahead, to the right of their car. She saw it again beside the car, then on the right, then behind, and again to the right as they drove past. Maggie strained to see what had caused the yellow flash but the balls were too thick. It only resembled the flash of lightning in a far away storm.

"What was that?" asked Maggie.

Father was still locked onto the road. " I have no idea." he replied flatly.

Maggie jerked her head back with the hope of seeing something, anything, other than bouncing balls of cotton. She peered back for several moments but saw nothing. She let out a defeated sigh. Then, from somewhere behind, a faint yellow flash glowed and illuminated a small patch of cotton balls. The yellow flashed again, this time brighter and larger.

"Dad! Something's behind us!" exclaimed Maggie.

He did not lift his eyes from the road for a second. "Oh. Okay," he drawled. "I hope that's a good thing."

The yellow flashed again. It was nearly upon the rear of the vehicle. Still Maggie could only see cotton balls bouncing over the rear of their car. She couldn't explain how, but the cotton balls were doing belligerent things in front of whatever was behind her. They erupted in all directions away from it as if being blasted out of a cannon. The yellow flashed again. It was still coming closer and was now in the passing lane beside them. This time she could make out something amidst the torrent of puffs. She could see the side of a vehicle in the passing lane. The flashing yellow was a hazard light.

"Dad it's the police!" cheered Maggie.

Father was still too focused on the road to celebrate. "Okay," he drawled again, "I hope they're here to help us."

Maggie watched the police vehicle as it slowly sped in front of her. It was a large truck with a huge, dark windshield. The police truck had a massive angular frame and rode high above the ground. Due to its bulky mass, Maggie thought it was more appropriate as a military personnel carrier, or even a tank, than a police truck. It's large, heavily treaded tires rumbled past them in the adjacent lane. Maggie inspected it's paint job. It was sportingly striped black and yellow, like a hornet. She could just barely make out a round emblem on its side door which read, "*Cotton Ball County Sheriff's Department.*"

"I'd say they're locals," said Maggie absently.

"What's that?" chimed Father.

"Oh, uh, nothing Dad," replied Maggie. She was too focused on the oddity traveling beside them. In the bed of the truck, securely built up against the cab, was a large piece of machinery, similar in form and size to an air conditioning unit, except there were bolts, and pipes and wires attached all around it. "Perhaps it's a generator of some kind?" she thought. From the generator attached a large, wide, flexible tube that ran on top of the cab and ended above the windshield. Maggie focused on the apparatus. The truck was now passing them. "It's a blower," she said in awe.

It was, in fact, a blower, and working quite well. With the blower in operation, the cotton balls were diverted away from the front of the police truck, as if an invisible wall was in front of it, dispersing cotton balls in all directions, like water spouting from a whale's blowhole. With the blower in operation, it also allowed the police truck to have visible clearance towards where it was headed.

The truck traveled a short distance in front of them, and then matched their speed. Father finally glanced over at the vehicle. "Why I do believe we are being rescued?" he exclaimed.

Maggie clapped her hands together and fidgeted restlessly in her seat. She hopped about as the police truck flashed its turn signal and gradually veered in front of them. The intensity of cotton balls worsened as they deflected away from the truck and onto the car. This lasted only briefly as the truck merged more and more into their lane. The cotton balls quickly decreased in numbers, at least from directly in front. Father and Maggie could now see the road in front of them.

"Sweet relief!" cheered Father.

Maggie clapped and giggled excitedly. She smiled wide and lovingly at her rescue truck. The truck was now positioned correctly and steadied itself in front them. Without hesitation a loudspeaker sounded, "This is Cotton Ball County Sheriff's Department. Please remain calm. Do not attempt to pass this vehicle. You are to follow until instructed otherwise. Flash your high beams to signal your compliance."

Father quickly flashed his high beams in response. With the Sheriff in front of them, the mood inside the cab quickly changed from paranoia to positivity. "Dad we're gonna make it," Maggie exclaimed.

"I know Sweetie! This is fantastic," replied Father. The car fell to an exuberant quiet as they confidently watched the truck in front of them. Cotton balls scattered in all directions as the two vehicles marched down the highway. It was quite a spectacle. Maggie and her father had front row seats.

Being behind the behemoth of a truck trudging through the torrent of cotton took on a feeling that Maggie had never felt before. She felt as though she was at the helm of a ship, forging it's way across a dangerous sea. The balls of cotton were like enormous walls of white water. The sheriff's truck was the bow of the ship, pointed into the storm. The bow was stronger than the storm. It muscled its way onward. The waves of cotton balls crested and crashed away from the ship. Maggie knew she could weather the storm.

It wasn't too long before the loud speaker barked back to life startling Maggie from her daydream. "We will be exiting the highway. Follow this vehicle. Do not stop until you have been instructed to do so. Flash your lights to signal your compliance."

Father flashed his lights in response. "I wonder where they're taking us?" pondered Maggie.

Father was still as focused as he had been when the trouble first began. Without taking his eyes off of the road, he cocked his head slightly towards Maggie. "My guess is to that rest stop that was on your GPS."

Maggie had forgotten all about her GPS. She glanced around her sides and at her feet for the lost article. She felt all around in the blind spots beneath and behind her. Still, she felt nothing. She reached far back at the floorboard behind her and her muscles stretch painfully as she exerted herself. "I need to stretch," she groaned. It wasn't until she raised one leg to reach farther back when she felt something fall from her seat and bounce against her calf. It landed at her feet with a thud. She knew what it was.

"Yes!" she said triumphantly. She snatched up the fallen device and turned on the screen. It only took a moment to figure out where they were. "Yep! We're at the rest stop," she said confidently.

"Good," replied Father.

Maggie looked up from the small screen. They were still following the truck at a slow speed. The cotton ball storm was unrelenting. Visibility was still heavily skewed except for in between them and their rescuer. The truck turned to the right somewhat sharply, recovered and then turned sharply to the left. Father followed the truck with precision. The Sheriff's vehicle slowed to a snail's pace. The loud speaker blared again, "Prepare to stop. Signal your compliance."

Father flashed his high beams. The car was now barely moving at all. "Stop," blared the loud speaker. Father stopped the car. Strong winds jostled the two vehicles as they idled.

"You are at Cotton Ball County Rest Stop," sounded the loud speaker. "You are safe here. Do not attempt to drive any further. Do not exit your vehicle until the storm has subsided unless it is an absolute emergency. National Weather Service has issued a cotton storm warning for much of the county. The storm is expected to subside after nightfall. Do you comply?"

Father flashed his high beams once more. The truck immediately rumbled away. Maggie was surprised at how quickly the yellow flashing lights dimmed into the blizzard of white puffs. Although the truck appeared very far away she could still distinctly feel the rumble of its large engine. She followed the flashing light until it became barely visible. With the two travelers now safely parked, it was somewhat humorous to watch their savior cast away, back into oblivion. Maggie focused on the dim glow of yellow that was barely visible. It traveled slightly to the right, then strongly to the left for a short time. Then the yellow flash, once again, became brighter, and brighter.

"Dad they're coming back around," exclaimed Maggie.

"They probably had to make a u-turn to get back on the highway," thought Father aloud.

The flashing, once again, became very bright. Cotton balls again intensified tremendously as the truck barreled close to them once more. The rumble of the truck's heavy engine vibrated the floor board of their small car. She could hear the howl of the blower, whistling out a continuous blast of air.

The front of the truck emerged through the billowing cotton. It was large and angular like the rest of the body. Large, square headlights dimly lit in front. The grill resembled that of a semi truck, muscular and cold, built for wear and tear with no regard for fashionability. Maggie and Father warmly raised their sights up to the cab of the truck. They wanted to put a face to their hero. They wanted to thank the brave public servants who risked their lives to save them. Their expressions quickly changed from confirming to confusion as they tried to peer through the windshield of the sheriff's truck. The windows were completely black. They could see nothing through the blacked out glass.

Maggie and her father gawked, mouths ajar, as the massive vehicle lumbered by without even a hesitation in its stride. It's massive, treaded tires, rolling like tank treads, moved the vehicle slowly beside them, and then behind them. Maggie lifted herself from her seat and turned to watch the vehicle as cotton balls once again began to white out her field of view. Within moments, the dimming yellow flasher was the only remaining evidence of what had just transpired.

Maggie and her father spent the rest of the late afternoon waiting out the storm of tumbling cotton balls. They replayed the entire ordeal excitedly trying to understand how they had gotten saved. They wondered if they were the only ones to make it to safety and if other vehicles had been spared as they had, by the big, blowing, armoured vehicle with blacked out windows. They chatted and pondered intermittently, and tracked the progression of the setting sun through the blanketing puffs of cotton.

Watching a sunset through a cotton ball storm is a very uneventful affair. There are three colors involved. First there is white. Then as the sun sets it becomes gray. Then the gray fades to black. Maggie and her father sat in silence in the blackness. They had exhausted their conversations for the time being. They were still just as curious about their rescuer as they had been when it rumbled away hours earlier.

CHAPTER

11

Maggie jolted upright in her seat. She sat rigid and alert. Her breath was shallow and sporadic. She listened attentively. "What woke me up?" she thought. "I don't remember falling asleep. How long have I been asleep?"

She looked around and listened intently as she replayed the actions that had brought her to where she was. She could neither see, nor hear anything that would have awoken her. It was still very dark outside of the cab.

"Stars!" she exclaimed under her breath. For the first time in hours, Maggie could see her surroundings clearly. The horizon was, more or less, dark and flat in all directions. Father snored loudly next to her.

"Wow!" she thought to herself. "Maybe Dad's snoring is what woke me up." Whatever the reason, Maggie was now wide awake and had no desire to fall back asleep. Her body was stiff from the many hours traveling and being forced to seek refuge in the car. "I know it's dark but I have to go outside. My back is stiff. I feel like every joint in my body won't bend. I need to get out of this car," she thought. "I hope I don't wake up Dad."

Maggie slipped on her socks that had been wedged into her shoes below her. Her body strained as she bent forward to lace up her shoes. She tried not to shake the car as she prepared to exit it. She reached back behind and grabbed her windbreaker, slipped it on and zipped it up. Then reached up at the interior light above her and flipped it off so that it would not activate once she opened the door. She looked at her father. He was completely reclined in his seat, eyes shut, mouth agape and held slightly to the side. His breaths were deep. He must have been exhausted from the stress of driving through the cotton storm earlier. In the starlight, Maggie could see her father's profile. His facial hair had stubbled out noticeably. A few more days and he would have a full on beard. Maggie chuckled at the notion. She had never even considered her father with a beard. He was handsome enough without one. "You need to shave Dad," she whispered humorously. And with that, she opened the car door and, more or less, silently slipped out of the car.

Outside was distinctly colder than inside the car. The forceful wind that had summoned the maelstrom of cotton balls was now nothing more than a crisp, cool breeze. Maggie shivered a little but the feeling of the wind was fine. It was a steady wind that didn't lessen or strengthen in intensity. It did not waver in the direction that it traveled either. It gently howled in her ears. It was, very much, the same wind that she had encountered when she was atop The Great Summit, days earlier, looking out across hill country and the land of reservoirs. She inhaled deeply and faced the wind. She closed her eyes. The wind whispered to her the secrets of the mountains. It kissed her cheeks with the blessings of snow capped peaks. It filled her lungs with the grandeur of alpine vistas. She thought of Yellowsemite. She exhaled deeply and opened her eyes.

The mountains were nowhere in sight. The Grey Flat Desert streched out far and wide, until it met with the night sky. Flat, starkly flat, there wasn't even a tree or a bush to obstruct the horizon. Maggie momentarily decided to give up on romanticising about the majesty of Yellowsemite and instead turn her attention to the sky above.

"Wow," she said aloud. Never in her entire life had she seen a night so clear. The stars shone brightly above her. They were innumerable. Some were quite large, others were barely a pinprick in the black matte of night sky. They glistened and twinkled, in every color of the spectrum. Orange, and purple, and blue and green, some even seemed to change colors as would crystals hanging from a chandelier. Maggie was bedazzled. Her hands dangled loosely at her sides. She arched her neck far back so as to only see the night sky. It was immense and breathtaking. There was no moon. There were no city lights on the horizon. There wasn't any pollution in the air. The only light provided was that which burned light years away. It was perfect. It was as if Maggie could reach out into the black tree of night and pluck its starry fruit with her fingers. Maggie thought about that and chuckled sheepishly at the notion.

Her neck was starting to hurt, as it had certainly not been used in such a way since her travels began, so she decided it best to lay upon the ground. She stiffly lowered herself and laid down on the earth. The ground was surprising soft, alarmingly soft. Maggie let her fingers touch the ground. It felt as if she was rubbing her shirt.

"What the...?" she said aloud. She rolled over to inspect the ground. "No way," she gawked. The ground had a fine layer of sinuous cotton covering it. Not very deep at all, a layer of cotton blanketed the ground all around her, but was very thin, like outdoor carpeting.
"That makes sense," said Maggie in a tone as if she was stating the obvious. She had personally witnessed cotton balls the size of tumbleweeds blanket her surroundings in catastrophic proportions. They had to leave some kind of evidence. She looked around to see if the cotton had amassed anywhere else. That was when she noticed that she wasn't alone.

Several other cars were parked next to hers. In the darkness she squinted in earnest to try and take in her immediate surroundings. She counted ten or so glistening wind shields randomly parked in an area the size of an olympic sized swimming pool. At the far edge of the pool, was a large mound. She wanted to investigate the mound but there were too many cars in the way. She actually felt a little dumb that she had not thoroughly investigated her surroundings when she first got out the car.

The cool breeze picked up in intensity for a moment. Maggie shivered as it chilled her. "Better get back inside," she thought. She looked down at the soft bed of cotton below her, stood up, and then turned and walked a few steps back to her car, went inside and quickly fell asleep.

Maggie awoke to a rumbling outside of the car. She opened her eyes. The cab was dimly lit from the outside. The inside of the windshield and windows were beaded with condensation caused by a night of harboring sleeping occupants. It wasn't quite daybreak, but the stars that had shone so brilliantly the night before were nowhere to be seen. She looked over at her father. He was nowhere to be found. Maggie shot up from her seat startled. The rumble grew louder. She looked all around but could see very little outside due to the foggy windshield. She began to panic. Just as she was about to sound the horn by pressing on the steering wheel she noticed a note attached to it. She quickly grabbed it and read aloud, "Went to take a shower. Don't go wandering." Maggie looked up perplexed thinking, "Where on earth is he going to find a shower out here?"

Maggie levered her seat back into an upright position, slipped on her shoes and stepped outside. The air was still and cool. There was no longer any breeze. She quickly looked about to locate her father. From across the olympic sized swimming pool of a parking lot she saw a clean shaven version of him walking towards her from the mound of cotton. Her relief was short-lived as the rumbling of a large heavy engine alerted her attention elsewhere. Maggie turned around to, once again, see the large and overbearing, somewhat menacing, grill of the sheriff's vehicle that had rescued them from the storm of cotton balls. The large truck treaded laboriously and stopped a short distance from her. Maggie tried to peer through the blacked out windshield. Even in the early morning light she was unable to see anything inside the cab. For a moment, the engine idled steadily. Maggie's feet vibrated on the cotton linened land. Her toes chattered within her shoes and tickled her to a degree that was obnoxious and uncomfortable.

After what seemed like an eternity, the engine powered down and quieted. The ground steadied and returned to its normal motionless state.

Maggie just stood there looking up at the monstrosity that, for no apparent reason, decided to slumber at her feet. The driver's side door popped open with a loud metal "skreek". A pair of small, shiny leather boots briefly dangled into view, and then dropped to the ground gracefully, skipping the safety step. The petite frame of a long haired woman, dressed in a well manicured, tight fitting uniform slammed the door to the truck and striped confidently towards Maggie.

"G'mornin!" chimed the female officer. Her tone was pleasant, and deliberate.

Maggie was visibly dumbfounded at the paradox she had just witnessed. "Uhh… good morning?" forced Maggie.

"Good morning officer," replied Father.

Maggie jolted to her side and looked up at him. Somehow, he managed to stand right beside Maggie without her taking notice. He had shaved, and bathed. To Maggie, he looked nothing like the scruffy, haggard man she had shared a car cab with for the last few days. His hair was slicked back, and still wet from his apparent shower. His clothes were clean and wrinkle free. Maggie couldn't help but lean in to smell him. He smelled like jasmine and eucalyptus.

"Sheriff Caldwell," the officer corrected.

"Sheriff Caldwell," parroted Father.

"So, were you folks able to make the best of things last night?" asked the Sheriff. The woman was definitely on the clock. From her tone and presentation, Maggie surmised that the Sheriff was making sure there were no unattended emergencies that had gone unreported during the night.

"We were," replied Father. "thanks to whoever rescued us on the highway last night, we are going to be just fine."

Maggie couldn't help but inspect the female Sheriff. She was tiny. She could only weigh about 20 lbs more than Maggie and was an inch taller, if that. Sheriff Caldwell gave away nothing to suggest that she was small though. She was tough, and fearless. She looked like she could skin the hide off of a wild russian boar that was still alive, but she was also undeniably beautiful. If there was a modeling line for officers in uniform, Sheriff Caldwell would have been the headliner. Maggie immediately took a liking to her. "It was you," said Maggie. "You brought us here last night."

Sheriff Caldwell glanced at Maggie. She was obviously humored by Maggie's blunt accusation, but she neither confirmed nor denied it. "I'm a part of the Storm Division. It's my job to make sure that those caught in the middle of one are brought to safety. Yesterday's storm was a bad one. Totally blew our forecasts out of the water. When I started my shift the storm was sixty miles ahead of me. You two were the last ones on the highway. When I got radioed that you were en route, the storm had already passed my station." Caldwell scuffed the ground with her spotless black leather boot and looked away. "We try to do our rescues in front of the storm. Not in it."

The group fell silent. Maggie looked back at the truck. "How can you see where you're going with it being so dark in there?" she asked, gesturing towards the cab.

Sheriff Caldwell looked back at Maggie and let out a smirk that revealed the faintest hint of pearly white teeth that undoubtedly contributed to a dazzling smile. She looked at Maggie without saying a word. She turned around on a dime and started walking back to the massive vehicle. "You coming?" she said at last without breaking stride.

Maggie smiled wide and looked up at her father. He looked caught off guard and stuttered a little before answering, "Uh, why are you asking me? You didn't ask me yesterday when you ran off," he chided. Maggie ran after the sheriff as if she was late for her first day of school. The sheriff stepped up and opened the heavy driver's side door. Maggie caught up to Caldwell in no time and was breathing heavily at her side. She looked up into the cab. Caldwell looked at Maggie.

"You gonna climb in or what?" asked the sheriff.

Maggie was giddy with excitement as she clambered up inside of the dark cab. Maggie positioned herself appropriately on the large and comfortable bench seat. She looked back down at Sheriff Caldwell and slid to the other side of the cab. Caldwell reached up to a handle at the base of the seat and hopped up onto it with the skill and precision of a ballerina performing a pirouette.

As Maggie was getting herself seated, "Sheriff Caldwell!" yelled a familiar voice from outside of the cab. Caldwell leaned back to see who was calling her name. Maggie did the same. The only problem was that the windows were not only blacked out from the outside, but also from the inside. Maggie stretched closer to Caldwell to see what the commotion was about. Father was waving his arms and holding on to a fine mesh of cotton that has accumulated on the radiator of the car.

"Hang tight kid," speaking to Maggie, the sheriff said firmly "and Shawn don't even think about coming up front." Caldwell looked at the ground suspiciously and shook her head as if she already knew she was making the wrong decision. Maggie watched Caldwell march back to her dad with the same degree of urgency that she displayed from their initial encounter. Maggie relaxed against the seat in near darkness, except for the open door.

Without warning an overhead light turned on, "What'd you get in trouble for?" Asked a young male voice from behind her.

Maggie screamed as if she had been accosted walking down a dark alley. She ducked below the seat cushion and pinned herself down against the floorboard. "Don't touch me!" She warned.

"Woah, woah. Take it easy. I'm not gonna hurt you," consoled the strange voice. A young boy popped his head over the seat to reveal himself. The boy was handsome. He had a slender face and a strong chin. His hair was dark brown and cut short at the sideburns, gradually lengthening into a short curly mat on top. He had clear blue eyes that penetrated deeply into anything that he looked upon.

Maggie looked at the boy with accusing eyes that screamed at him with embarrasment and frustration. "That! Was not funny!" she denounced.

"Uhh... sorry?" Said the boy, "I've been stuck inside this truck all night and haven't had anyone except my MOM to talk to."

Maggie eyed the boy suspiciously "She's your mom?"

The boy looked at Maggie squarly in her eyes, shrugged his shoulders and spoke plainly, "Yeah, I might of gotten kicked out of English yesterday at school. I live with my mom so she had to come pick me up."

Maggie's eyes flashed with interest. She subconciously bit her lip and slowly squirmed out of her sheltered nook to reposition herself on the front bench seat. As she settled herself, Maggie took a quick glance at Father who was fully engaged in conversation with Sheriff Caldwell. They were not going to be finished talking any time soon. The boy rested with his arms folded on the backrest waiting patiently for Maggie to get resettled. "That's better," said Maggie at last.

"Yeah," said the boy, "I scared you so bad, I thought I was going to get arrested again."

Maggie chuckled, quickly shaking off her discomfort "Haha. So, she's your mom? Or you got arrested? Or you got arrested by your mom?" retorted Maggie. She would not be intimidated so easily.

The boy withdrew himself from the backrest and eyed Maggie with equal suspicion. "Not that it's any of your business, but yeah, I got picked up from school yesterday 'cause I took an assignment too literally." Maggie raised an eyebrow skeptically at the boy. "Look," he continued "all I did was show up in character for the reading of Hamlet, but since I've already been "warned" by the hall moniters about my (holding up two fingers from both hands) "antics", they called my mom and sent me home. Then that stupid cotton storm hit and I HAD to go with her 'cause she was (raising the same two fingers from each hand) "on call". The boy blew a loud exhale of resentment as he withdrew from Maggie and looked away, shaking his head.

Maggie looked the boy over from the corner of her eyes. She couldn't help but reveal a humored smirk as he showed the disapproval of his untimely punishment. "So, shouldn't you be out of school by now?" she asked.

He cleared his throat at the question, "I have year round school. It's the pits. I can't wait 'til I go to high school. Anyways," he continued "I've been stuck in the back of this stupid cab all night and YES, she is going to drop me off back at school in about an hour." The boy looked down at the floorboard and shook his head in disbelief and defiance.

Maggie squinted at the boy and smiled broadly. Her faced was alit with humored intrigue. "I'm Maggie," she said holding out her hand.

"Shawn," said the boy holding out his "but my friends call me 'Slim'. Nice to meet you Maggie." He took Maggie's hand and shook it sincerely. Maggie once again eyed Shawn suspiciously. Shawn could tell his nickname confused her, "It's a long story," he said with a shrug.

The truck shook abruptly as Caldwell quickly hopped up into the cab. "Slim! Set your butt back there and don't say a word!" commanded Caldwell.

Shawn shut his mouth tightly and disappeared back out of sight. He winked at Maggie as he withdrew. Maggie looked away as her cheeks flushed pink with flattery. She bit her lip and looked away out the passenger window. The only problem was that she couldn't see out of the passenger window. Instead she only saw her reflection, an embarrassed reflection at that.

"Im sorry you had to meet my son like this. One day, hopefully, I'll be able to introduce him to nice girls like you. Bye Shawn." said the sheriff sarcastically. She pushed a nondesript button on the door panel. Instantly, a thick pane of glass raised up from the backrest, sealing the front half of the truck from the back half. Maggie and the sheriff looked at eachother without speaking. The sheriff winked at Maggie without making any other expressions as if to tell Maggie, "Don't worry, he'll be fine."

Maggie couldn't help but giggle.

"Want to see something cool?" prodded Caldwell.

Maggie didn't think she could be anymore entertained but invited the challenge anyway, "Um, sure?"

"Lights on!" spoke the sheriff. Instantly, the cab became illuminated with soft green light. Maggie looked around in disbelief. Every knob, dial, instrument, gauge (there were many) glowed a warm green. The door handles and window controls were easily visible and glowed in green. Even the fire extinguisher and emergency kit, fastened above her, were clearly visible in the green lighting. The cab was clean too, spotless.

"Wow," said Maggie as she looked around in awe.

Sheriff Caldwell seemed unimpressed and began typing on a keyboard that was built into the top of the dashboard. Without looking away from the keyboard she muttered, "Yeah, the technician said that the green would show everything in the cab real good. And that any dirt would show up too."

Maggie began looking for dirt on the floor board. She could see where her shoes had left little grains of dirt from where she had shuffled into her current position. "Oh my, I'm sorry I had no idea..." Maggie was mortified.

Caldwell looked over and stopped her in her tracks, "Don't worry about it kid." Caldwell looked at Maggie the way a doctor might study a new patient. She exhaled a little. "Here, check this out. Screen on," she commanded clearly.

Instantly, the windshield and windows came to life. Everything outside of the truck became visible. Maggie dropped her jaws and leaned forward in disbelief.

"This is incredible," was all she said under her breath.

The windshield was indeed a screen, displaying everything outside exactly as it appeared, except without color. Everything was clearly visible, but only in defined shades of gray, like a professional black and white photograph. Maggie could see the detailed outline of all the cars, along with the gravel in the parking lot. She could see a building at the far end of the parking lot, it was a bathroom.

"That's how Dad got so clean," declared Maggie. "That building was covered in cotton a minute a go. Did somebody clean it up?"

"Nope, it's still covered in cotton," replied Caldwell. "The windshield is a computer screen. We were having too much trouble trying to help people during the cotton storms. It was like the blind leading the blind, you know what I mean? We decided to go all electronic a few years ago. What your looking at is like a combination of infrared, radar and high resolution cameras. There's an instrument up on top of the roof that detects our surroundings in all directions. It gives distance away from objects, moving speed and bearing of other objects, size of objects and a whole bunch of other things too."

She touched a button that was built onto the steering wheel. A series of numbers displayed above and to the right of each object on the screen.

"See?" demonstrated Caldwell.

"That's incredible!" proclaimed Maggie. "So what happens when you're driving?" she asked.

"The same thing," replied Caldwell flatly. "This display shows real time with basically no delay. We see what is happening, as it's happening, even when no one else can. I can zoom in on objects within two miles distance." The Sheriff placed one finger from each hand on the screen and made a couple brief and precise movements against the glass. Suddenly the bathroom filled the screen. "See?" sheriff Caldwell continued with the tour, "This baby has a doppler weather station in the back so we get detailed weather information wherever we go. We also can link up with our aerial support team and other scarabs. And let's not forget about the most important thing on the truck, the blower."

Maggie was practically dumbfounded by all of the information she was processing. She furrowed her brow and looked absently in front of her, obviously internalizing. "Sheriff, what are scarabs?" she asked.

Caldwell looked at Maggie boastfully and in a tone that could not help but be proud, replied, "Honey, you're in one." Caldwell turned her head forward to the horizon and chimed confidently, "Toughest thing in the desert."

"Wow," said Maggie. She was mystified. "I want to drive one when I grow up."

"Oh yeah?" sounded Caldwell.

"Yeah," snapped Maggie. "This thing is awesome. Drive around in storms and save people. You have the best job ever."

Caldwell stared pensively at Maggie, unaware that she was holding her breath. She snapped her head forward and stared out past the vast expanse of flat, barren earth. The sun was beginning to rise. Caldwell stared out, poised in perfect posture, alert and ready, and at the same time caught off guard.

At last she spoke, "You know kid, there are weeks that go by when I don't even see a car on the highway. This grey chunk of land and the random cotton storms that pop up are job security. I go home to my desert shack each night and look at the stars, and watch night hawks chase bugs in the sky, and I think, "Can I do this as my career for the rest of my life?" she paused, "It's quiet out here, real quiet. Sometimes it can get plain lonely. Sometimes I wonder, if things had gone another way..."

Caldwell stared out transfixed within her thoughts. Maggie looked up at her, listening intently to each of the Sheriff's thoughts.

"Don't give in kid," said the Sheriff. "When the time comes for you to live, you run for it. And don't look back. There's going to come a time when the world doesn't seem so warm and fuzzy. It's going to test you and challenge you, and try to break you. Don't give in."

Maggie reflected on the sheriff's words. She had no idea what had prompted such brutal honesty. Yet given the recent inexplicable events that had happened to her while traveling, Maggie felt she understood Caldwell's words of wisdom. Maggie stared out into the horizon, deep in thought.

"When I was growing up, well I mean I'm still growing up but," started Maggie, "when I was younger, I wanted to be just like my dad." Maggie smiled contently, "But I feel different now. I don't think I *can* be like Dad," Maggie outstretched her arms with palms cupped upward, as if weighing the needs of her father with the needs of her own on a scale. Caldwell watched Maggie intently. A spark of excitement lit upon her face. Maggie looked at her hands without speaking, she stared at them, pondering what things she might do with them. At last, maggie let out a deep and satisfying breath and said with a smile, "I will just be me."

Caldwell grinned proudly.

The two sat in silence. Maggie took her gaze away from Caldwell and reflected on the Sheriff's words of wisdom. Caldwell looked outside resolutely. Eventually, enough time had passed that Maggie had forgotten she was still engaged in a conversation. When Caldwell spoke up, Maggie jumped a little in surprise. "Think your dad is trying to leave?" elucidated Caldwell.

Maggie, realizing she had abandoned her father, once again, started making attempts to exit the truck. "Oh my!" said Maggie. "I can't believe I just forgot about him. Thank you Sheriff. Thank you very much. I'd better help him get ready."

"Sounds like a plan kid," said Caldwell. "You can get out on the passenger side."

Without hesitating, Maggie opened the door and shuffled out. She hit the ground and was about to walk to her car when Sheriff Caldwell threw out a question. "Hey kid?" she called. Maggie turned around and looked up at the Sheriff's green glowing, illuminated face. "Where are you headed anyways?" asked Caldwell.

"Yellowsemite," replied Maggie, "It's my first time."

Caldwell cracked a smile and replied. "That sounds nice. Just a few more hours across this desert and you should get there. You might even make it with time to explore."

At first, Maggie smiled wide at the news, but then withdrew her happiness. "What if there's another cotton storm?" she asked. The stressful events that unfolded yesterday were still very fresh in her mind.

Caldwell chuckled and replied, "I think you will be just fine. The forecast is clear and calm. I don't think there's a snowball's chance of a cotton storm today."

"Okay," said Maggie relieved at the news, "I like that answer." Maggie again looked up at the sheriff. "Thank you for showing me your scarab Sheriff. "

"No problem kid," replied the sheriff. "Get there safe and would you mind closing the door for me?"

"Sure thing, and BYE SHAWN!!" Yelled Maggie. And with that, she closed the heavy door and walked a few steps to her car chuckling to herself in disbelief. Behind her, the massive engine of the truck rumbled back to life and began rolling towards the next car in the parking lot.

In front of her, Father looked at her sideways with a degree of concern on his face. "Who's Shawn?" he interrogated.

Maggie was caught red handed. She quickly recovered and played it cool, "Shawn? Nobody Dad, just her son. The Sheriff has to drop him off at school. That's all."

Father crossed his arms and eyed her suspiciously. "Uh huh," he said skeptically.

CHAPTER

12

The weather was nice. Maggie and Father were getting along amicably. Yellowsemite was within striking distance, and Maggie was clean, comfortably clean. Father made sure to allow time for Maggie to properly wash before getting in the car. Something about driving the entire day before, and then having to spend the night in the car must have alerted him to the lack of sanitation that was occurring during their travels. In any event, the rusted, leaky, dribbling excuse for a shower had done nothing less than cleanse Maggie's soul. It's unfiltered, rotten egg smelling water spread like room temp butter over crispy toast. The hot water heater in that little shack of a public restroom was a dandy. The water was scalding hot and steamed up the small, tinted, cobweb covered, sliding window above her that served more as a skylight than a view.

Such is the life of a traveler. One must take what comes across one's path and make the most of it. The luxuries of home are so often overlooked, or taken for granted. They become scarce and coveted when traveling. Maggie wished for a real shower. She wished for her bed, but above all else, she wanted to reach her destination. The excitement of exploring and the anticipation of adventure guided her interests farther and farther away from the comforts of home.

The expanse of the Flat Grey Dirt Desert splayed out in all directions. The land was flat. The land was grey. The land was absolutely a barren, desolate desert. Maggie's father could have read a book while driving if he had preferred. Maggie had exhausted her books. She had her fill with driving and reading. She was ready to explore with her hands and her feet, not within the confines of a packed little car. The terrifying vision she had experienced at the start of her journey had lost its intensity. It felt less like a threat and more like a memory. She was not as perplexed by it either. She did not understand why Johnny Muur told her "the river gives and the river takes" in the dream. She did not understand why Bart, the toothless old man told her the same thing either. Nor did she understand why Johnny wrote the same statement at the end of his book. Maggie had exhausted herself trying to understand the meaning. She was done grinding her thoughts over the matter. "I don't know what it means, and I really don't care," she thought to herself. She smiled approvingly as if she had just reached a hard fought stalemate against a worthy opponent at a game of chess.

Maggie stared off into the vast expanse of The Grey Dirt Desert. The morning had progressed into an ideal day. The sky had a dark blue tinge to it. Last night's pummeling winds seemed to have no aftereffects as there was no dust or pollution in the air. Maggie could see far off into the horizon. The land was so flat and the sky was so clear she thought she could see the roundness of Earth.

"It's so flat," said Maggie inviting conversation.

"Yep," replied Father as he reached for his thermos of coffee. He took a sip and set the thermos back in its cup holder in the center console. He looked back up at the road ahead and put his hand lazily on the steering wheel and chuckled absently. "They weren't lying when they named this place, 'Flat, Grey, Dirt Desert.' Ha!" he laughed aloud.

Maggie chuckled jovially along with her father until they both fell into an engaged silence.

"Dad?" asked Maggie after a few moments of listening to the monotonous, yet melodic, sounds of tires and engine moving over the well paved highway.

"Yeah Sweetie?" replied Father softly.

"So when was the last time you went to Yellowsemite?" she asked.

Father shifted in his seat and scratched the back of his head. Doing so made him look a little uncomfortable. "Well I've only been there once actually, with my parents. When I was your age. We had the best time! It was so beautiful." he said in reminiscence.

"What'd you guys do?" asked Maggie.

Father continued to look ahead and smiled absently. "We ahh, we went hiking, and fishing, and swimming. I remember riding bikes, and camping. I remember being surrounded by enormous rocky mountains that were capped with snow. I remember walking through fields of wildflowers of all kinds of colors. We uh, we saw lots of wildlife all over the place." He paused as if reflecting on something very important, "I... I just remember feeling so small, you know? For the first time in my life I wasn't the center of attention. It was an amazing feeling, like everything around me was more important than myself. I had never felt that way before." He paused again to think about his next words, "It was like, the world didn't need me. At home, my parents needed me. My teachers needed me at school. I knew that one day even my town would need me, at least for working and paying taxes. But not this place. Yellowsemite didn't need me. I was just like a, like a spectator, you know? Everywhere we went, life was thriving, and it was beautiful, and, majestic. And I had nothing to do with it. I was just lucky that such a place existed." He paused and held his breath. He stared ahead into the distance. His mouth was slightly ajar, "I've never felt that way anywhere else." He exhaled loudly as if he had just admitted to something he had never told anyone before."

"Wow Dad!" remarked Maggie, "That sounds awesome."

"It is awesome Maggie," said Father with a hoarse voice. His tone had changed. It was a little tense. He squeezed the steering wheel firmly and slid his grip back and forth with each hand ever so slightly.

Maggie had noticed the subtle changes in her father. To her, the cues were quite abrupt. It made Maggie feel a little uneasy. "What's gotten into him?" she thought. "He was totally fine a minute ago. Is he not telling me something? Why would he just change like that?" Maggie made a funny, inquisitive face towards her father. He paid no attention and stared ahead. Maggie ran her fingers through her wavy hair and looked once more out the window.

The sky was still brilliantly clear but a couple clouds had formed. They were small in size and relatively low to the ground. They looked like large, white puffs of popcorn. The popcorn clouds cast very crisp, distinct shadows on the flat desert floor. "I don't care if he's uncomfortable. I want to know more," she thought to herself.

"If Yellowsemite is so special to you, why didn't you ever go back?" asked Maggie as passively as she could.

Father didn't respond. He just kept driving.

Maggie didn't want to pester him, but she needed a response. "Dad?" asked Maggie sincerely.

"I heard you Maggie," said Father flatly. He exhaled loudly again, only this time his breath quivered a little. "I did try to go back once," swallowing "with you and your mother."

"You went with me and Mom!" exclaimed Maggie. "Oh that's so exciting."

"I said I tried!" interjected Father. "I, tried..." His face was strained with anxiety. He was obviously uncomfortable. He looked very sad.

Maggie was at a loss for words. She wanted to know more but he was obviously distraught. She just looked at him, watching, waiting for a reaction. Father just kept driving. She had never seen him like this before. He was always composed and thoughtful and patient. "Whatever happened must be very difficult for him," she thought.

"Brrrrrrrrrrrrrrrrrrrrrrrrrrrrrrrrrrrrrrr," shook the car. Maggie jolted upright and looked outside to see what was happening.

"What are you doing Dad?" asked Maggie, her voice quivered in fear. "You're driving us off the road!" Maggie looked back her father. His eyes were locked onto what he was doing. He continued to steer the car off the road, gradually decelerating. He said nothing as the car crackled and crumbled and rumbled over flat, grey dirt. Maggie looked at him as if he was a madman. She trusted that he would not put her in harm's way, but she also had no idea what he was doing. She looked around to see if any passersby were also witnessing this act of lunacy. She looked behind her to see large plumes of spiraling, grey dust billow out behind them, like a supersonic jet leaving contrails.

The car slowly came to a stop. Soon, the gravelly noise of the moving vehicle was replaced by squeaky brakes and an idling engine. The car had stopped. Grey dust caught up to the vehicle and completely obscured the view. Maggie instinctively coughed at the sight of the thick cloud enveloping the car's exterior. Father let the car idle. He just stared ahead. The dust slowly cleared. The low hanging popcorn clouds slowly drifted by. One cruised steadily overhead and blanketed the car in shadow. Father turned off the car. The two sat in silence.

Maggie was completely at a loss. Moments ago, she was headed to a wonderland of natural beauty having a great time with her companion. Now she sat motionless, afraid to move, for fear that her dad would perform another incredulous act if she dare say another word. Outside the dust slowly diluted into the clear midday air.

"Maggie," he said relentingly, "talking about your mother has never been easy for me," with a sigh. "But I know, I know that you are old enough… to know…" He rolled his tongue in between his jaws and looked away out the driver's window. He continued, "to know what happened."

Maggie was floored. She just sat there, looking up to him. Of course she had always wondered about what had happened, but he always found a way of weaseling out the situation. There were times, as a young girl, at the supermarket, or at the movie theater that a passing woman would ignite a flurry of questions like; "Is she my mom?" or "Is Mommy like her?" or as Maggie grew older, "Am I like my mom?". It didn't happen very often, but when it did, her father always had a way of pacifying the ordeal. At home, it was different though. Maggie knew he thought about her.

He would be washing dishes or performing some other routine chore. Maggie would watch him in secret. It was often after school on those comfortable afternoons when all was quiet and peaceful, he would stop whatever he was doing, and stare out of the nearest window. His body language gave the impression that he was expecting someone to walk up the front steps, someone he had waited a long time to see. After about a minute, he would drop his head, and continue the chore he was carrying out. Maggie knew he was expecting her. She just knew it.

"You were only two months old," he continued. His tone was quiet but firm. He seemed to have composed himself "and we decided, that since my job was getting transferred, and you and your mother were doing well, that we should take a trip, to Yellowsemite." He paused and put a closed fist up against his mouth, and looked away longingly. Maggie stared at him silently. The blue sky behind him was now devoid of any remaining dust particles. He exhaled and looked back at Maggie. He forced a painful smile and gazed upon her lovingly through eyes that wanted to cry, but refused to. He continued with the story, "We" coughing, "we decided to take the southern entrance. It follows along the river and is very scenic. We had just entered the park. We were driving along the river, in a section called the Grand River Canyon. It's..."

"Oh, I know about the river canyon!" interjected Maggie energetically. As if scripting from a travel guide, she recited, "The Grand River Canyon is the world's deepest river canyon. Inside of it, the Flowy River cuts through two mountain ranges. The Yellow Range, and the Semite Range." Maggie folded her arms confidently and pressed her lips into a sliver of a smile.

"Yes, Maggie, that is all true. Now if you don't mind, I'd like to finish my story." Father looked at Maggie skeptically. Maggie's ego had been humbled. Her cheeks flushed rosy pink. She smiled sheepishly and clasped her hands together. Father continued his story. "It was early afternoon. There were thunder clouds near us, but it wasn't cold. It was warm enough to have our windows rolled down. Your mother had her hair tied back with a handkerchief so it wouldn't blow in her face. You were in the back seat napping," he sighed deeply, "It was perfect." He looked away once more. "It was perfect," he sighed even deeper.

He looked back at Maggie. "We had just entered the canyon section. As you already know, it's very narrow and the road runs right beside the river, very scenic, but the river is very fast moving. Too fast to..." he stared blankly into nothing, "swim. As we drove farther into the canyon it began to rain. It rained hard. Very hard. In a couple of minutes it rained so hard we could barely see the road. There was no place to pull off and wait out the storm so we just kept going. I was very uncomfortable driving. But your mother wasn't. She was so brave and confident. She always was." Father pressed his lips together and looked at his daughter. He soothingly ran his fingers through her hair. He looked at her fondly.

"Go on Dad," said Maggie softly.

He set his hands on his thighs and squeezed them anxiously. He looked down and then away out the window. "At one point," he continued, "the road and the river make a wide bend. The river gets much wider and doesn't have any rapids or anything like that. It just widens and keeps flowing swiftly down the canyon. Anyways, we were passing that section when out of nowhere your mother screams out, 'Stop! There's a man out there!' I stopped the car and looked where she was pointing."

He paused and furrowed his brow. He shook his head jerkily. "I didn't see a man," he said emphatically. "With the rain pouring so heavily, I could barely make out the bank. We had stopped at a point where the river made a wide bend. The bank was sandy, arched out, and gently sloped out into the river. I could see a couple of boulders sticking out of the water beyond the bank. Sarah was pointing in that direction," he paused and sighed. "I told her I couldn't see anybody. 'He's right there,' she said. 'At the edge! Don't you see him?' I got out of the car, with the rain pouring down. I strained desperately to see something, anything, that resembled a man." He held up his hands in defeat. "I didn't see him... your mother tapped on the window to get my attention. She pointed on the glass, as if to motion that I go to him. I looked back and still saw nothing. I looked back at your mother like 'What do you want me to do?' Sarah shot out of the car and began running down to the river. 'He's going to drown!' she yelled as she ran to the river. 'Sarah no!' I yelled, 'there's nothing there,' she kept running. I ran after her but I wasn't fast enough. When she got to the water's edge she didn't stop. She waded out to the first boulder and climbed onto it. I pleaded to her, 'Sarah get back here! Please! Come back!' She turned back to me, 'I can get him!' she yelled back."

Father was breathing heavily. He had a confused, yet determined expression on his face. "I ran after your mother towards the river's edge. Even there, the water was swift. Your mother turned back to me and started to wade to the next boulder. Even at the edge of the water!" he thrust his arms out in front of him, "I couldn't see anyone else. I just kept yelling at her to 'turn around, turn around!' But she wouldn't listen. Then, from out of nowhere, a large log came drifting downstream. I yelled to her to get out of the way. It was heading straight for her. I jumped in the water to try and get to her." He paused and turned his face away from Maggie. His eyes were glazed over. He fought back the tears. "She was too far ahead of me," his voice was much quieter "I couldn't reach her in time. The log rolled in between the two boulders and crashed right into her. She never saw it coming. By the time she came up to the surface, she was already in the middle of the river. I wanted to jump in to save her, but I couldn't leave you Maggie..." He looked straight ahead and shook his head steadily. "I couldn't risk it," with clenched fists, "the current was too strong. I watched as your mother struggled to stay afloat as the current took her quickly downstream. I screamed for her to swim back." His voice trembled and then paused in desperation. He continued, "I ran back up onto the road, running as fast as I could to follow her. By the time I got to the car, she was out of sight." He drooped his shoulders and exhaled deeply. He spoke again quietly, "I turned the car around and followed the river searching for her. I searched, for hours, into the night." He stopped and bit his finger and looked deeply within. "At one point during the downpour...at one point," he stopped.

"Yeah Dad?" asked Maggie completely absorbed in his story.

He struggled to continue, "At one point I thought... I thought I saw" He looked as focused as ever, as though all of his concentration was bent on understanding what he was about to say. "A man," he said at last. "Through the downpour, I thought I saw an old man on the other side of the river." He ran his fingers through his hair. "I screamed and yelled for help, but I don't even think he saw me. I'm not even sure if I saw him." Father was now looking pensively at the floorboard below him. His lips were pressed together. He took a deep breath and exhaled slowly. He returned his gaze to Maggie. He looked much more composed and continued his story, "The park service searched for two weeks. They never found her." The car fell silent.

Maggie was surprisingly composed with hearing about the demise of her mother. She looked at her father. "Dad?" asked Maggie after a moment.

"Yeah Maggie?" said Father.

"Why are we going to that place?" she interrogated.

Father stirred in his seat restlessly. He seemed uncomfortable with the question. He rubbed his chin with the palm of his hand and looked ahead. "I have thought about this place everyday since I was a kid. It has given me inspiration, and wonder... and it has taken the love of my life," he said at last. "You're growing up so fast Maggie. And it's such a special place. But you deserve to see it. The valley, and the mountains, even the river." He turned and looked at Maggie confidently, piercingly.

He spoke at last, "There's going to come a time when the world won't seem as magical as it used to. It's going to feel small, and flat, and normal. And that isn't the best feeling, especially day in and day out. I won't be able to stop that Maggie. Only you can. Yellowsemite is inspiring. And it always will be. And even though I lost your mother there, it is still the best gift I can give to you. Better than money. Better than a car. Better than a house."

The car once again fell silent. Two travelers looked at each other warmly. Outside of the car, a popcorn cloud silently floated past the car, allowing sunlight to illuminate the cab. The Grey Dirt Desert laid out in all directions. Somewhere off in the horizon, a spectacular land beckoned adventure and exploration.

"You ready Maggers?" inquired Father.

Maggie stared out, as a whirlwind of thoughts and emotions flooded her mind. For some odd reason, Sheriff Caldwell's words came into her mind, *"When the time comes for you to live, you run for it. And don't look back. There's going to come a time when the world doesn't seem so warm and fuzzy. It's going to test you and challenge you, and try to break you. Don't give in."* Maggie smiled and nodded firmly, slowly, "Yeah Dad, I am."

Father started the engine. A blast of grey dust billowed away from the exhaust pipe. The car was shifted into gear, tires started rolling, and two travelers determinedly headed toward their destination.

CHAPTER

13

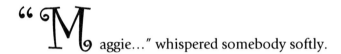"M aggie…" whispered somebody softly.

"Maggie" whispered the voice a little louder. Maggie smiled and chuckled absently.

"Maggie!" yelled a voice.

Maggie shot up, eyes blinking, looking about in all directions "Huh, what, I'm up, I'm up, I'm up Dad." Maggie stretched and moaned as she shook the sleep off of her. She yawned deeply and wiped some drool that was on the side of her mouth with the shoulder of her blouse. Once the ceremony of waking up was over, "Are we there yet?" she asked.

In his finest trucker accent Father replied, "Uhh, 10-4 Rubber Ducky."

Maggie smiled excitedly and looked around to absorb her surroundings. It was late in the day. "Dad? I thought we would make it earlier than this. What happened?" asked Maggie sincerely.

"I thought so too," he answered back. "We were making great time after the last gas station, but then we got held up by a motorhome. And I don't know why, but there wasn't a passing lane for like 2 hours."

Maggie shrugged her shoulders in dismissal. She expected to be immersed in the wonders of the park, but they were still in The Grey Dirt Desert, stopped behind a small line of cars. The only thing noteworthy about the land was that the desert was no longer flat. They were, in fact, headed into the trough of two small, rolling hills. From her vantage, Maggie could see several vehicles lined up in front of them. The cars idled, one in front of the other, all the way up to the crest of the hill. Atop the hill was a quaint, pleasant looking, wooden shack. She watched intently to understand what was happening. Each car seemed to stop there and hand something inside the shack. Then after a moment, a dainty, fair skinned arm would reach out from the shack and place something inside the parked vehicle, and then hand the driver some shiny documents. Sometimes the car would stop there a little longer and the dainty arms would point to some point of interest out in the distance beyond the ridge of the hill. Other times, the parked car would need no instructions and simply disappear over the ridge.

"Looks like they're getting tickets to a ride," said Maggie absently. Father said nothing but instead started moving about awkwardly. First he gently patted his shirt pocket, then his front jean pockets, and then he lifted himself from his seat and patted his rear pockets. "Where did I put my…?" he mumbled. Maggie watched with pure intrigue. He was obviously searching for his wallet. Maggie tried not to laugh out loud as she watched her father's subdued search become a frantic, confined inspection in the driver's seat of their small car. He looked like a malfunctioning, robotic chicken that was not capable of making complete movements. He shook the car as he wedged one arm down into the tight crevice between the seat and console. Then the other side. He stooped forward with both hands on the floorboard. The seat belt, locked into its safe mode and stopped his progress with a jerking "click". "Uhg," Father groaned in frustration.

"Dad," called Maggie.

"What?" responded Father preoccupied, still searching.

"Dad" repeated Maggie with greater emphasis.

"What!" repeated Father making it clear he did not want to be interrupted.

"You're holding up the line," revealed maggie.

Father looked up from his struggle and hesitated. "Ahh, yess…. Holding up the line." He rolled the car a couple of spaces forward until they were once again at an agreeable distance from the next car. Father returned to his missing wallet dance. He, once again, lifted himself out of his seat and jammed his fingers between the cushions behind him, to no avail. He was getting frantic.

"I'd better help him," thought Maggie. As much as she enjoyed her father's antics, she considered the possibility of actually not having money to get into the park. Perhaps more alarming, the inability to get home. Maggie calmly looked around the interior. It wasn't long before she settled her gaze on a very familiar dark, small, folded object tucked above the steering column, wedged in front of the instrument panel.

"Umm Dad?" requested Maggie.

Father looked up from where he had been reaching, far underneath the seat. He looked earnestly at Maggie, hoping she would alleviate his misfortune.

"Check the gas gauge," said Maggie flatly.

Father did so, and let out a victorious sigh of relief. "Great job Maggie. I was beginning to think that I had left it at the last gas station we stopped at. Thank you, seriously, thank you." The car once again returned to a relatively peaceful quiet as they awaited their turn to enter the park. Maggie looked ahead to see what advancement had been made.

The little hut was no longer in sight. It had been obscured by the last few cars in the front of the line. It was now a (hopefully) short waiting game. Maggie's stomach turned excitedly in anticipation. She ran a silent itinerary of all the sights she expected to see upon entry. She thought about the large, and unusual animals that she might stumble across along the numerous hiking trails she had read about. She checked her backpack to make sure all her vital supplies were accounted for and in their proper places. She smiled contently, feeling that all of her research and preparation would soon be gratified. She gazed at her reflection in the side view mirror. One bright flash of sunlight caught her off guard. She yanked her head back to see what had caused the flash.

It was the reflection of the sun glaring off of the windshield of a motorcycle. Behind the windshield was a leathery-skinned older man, with a large, dark, coarse beard, driving the machine. The motorcycle looked older, but unlike the sun beaten man, the bike was well cared for. It's handlebars had a smooth chrome finish, with long leathery straps that draped and dangled off of the tips. One large, round headlight was centered on the bike. It sparkled like a prism with each slight movement from the handlebars. A fat tear drop gas tank suspended the driver above the ground. It was painted eternal midnight black. Maggie was surprised she had not noticed the steady thunderous rumble caused by the small engine. Perhaps because they had been headed downhill since she had been awake. In any event, the man intrigued Maggie. "Why is he traveling all by himself?" she thought. "I wonder what it's like to travel on a motorcycle." She grimaced at the thought of having to go through a cotton ball storm protected only by a small rounded windshield. She smiled thinking about riding on one through the hill country and parking on the edge of The Great Summit. The man looked like a statue. Dark, shiny sunglasses, combined with his enormous beard, masked any facial expression that might reveal his current mood. "I don't think a bunch of cotton balls would affect that dude," she thought humorously. The little two cylinder sputtered to life as the procession of cars marched uphill, "Potatopotatopotatopotato."

Behind the leathery-skinned man was a very small car with large clear, windshields. Four adult passengers were crammed inside. Their heads looked to be touching the ceiling. It was uncomfortable just to see them amassed in such a small space. Maggie studied the face of each passenger. Each face was silent. No one speaking. Each pair of eyes locked forward, presumably awaiting admittance into the park. They looked healthy and fresh, but who in their right mind would travel across a bleak, flat, unchanging desert all the while crammed into an obviously uncomfortable position? "They must really want to be here," she thought. She studied their clothes and hairstyles. Maggie had never seen people like them before. "I wonder where they're from?" she thought. She looked at the front license plate for a clue. The plate was unfamiliar to her. It was very long and skinny, and did not say what state it hailed from. It had more symbols than any license plate she had ever seen as well. "Hmm" she thought "maybe they're from another country?"

As Maggie pondered the origins of the foreigners, something large rocked from side to side behind the small car. "There's the motorhome," she said scornfully.

It was, indeed, the slow moving motorhome that had kept them from reaching the park earlier in the day. The motorhome was big and boxy, far from old, but not new either. Maggie could see the passengers clearly above the small, tightly crammed, car in front of them. In the driver's seat was a skinny old man with a wrinkled forehead, balding scalp, thick white moustache and large bifocals. The man stared forward with both hands on the steering wheel. Beside him was a stout woman, who looked a little younger, wearing a bright blue shirt with pastel flowers printed on it. She was grinning wide and talking to somebody loudly, but it didn't appear to be the driver, as he was unchanging in his expression. While she turned her head and spoke, he only looked forward resolutely. Something dashed into view between the man and woman in the dark void between them that exposed the cavernous mass of the rest of the motorhome. It disappeared just as quickly as it had come into view. Maggie couldn't make out what it was but the motorhome once again shook wildly. This time it was the old man who spoke. Only his moustache indicated that he was talking. The white platform above his lips swayed and broadened as he conveyed his message. He finished talking, pressed his lips together firmly, and shook his head. From the darkness of the cabin emerged three small children, grinning wide from ear to ear. Their cheeks were flushed pink from prolonged activity. Two girls and a younger boy, all younger than ten years old. They were all chattering vivaciously at the same time. The elderly couple tried fervently to listen to each child, but from Maggie's perspective, it was obvious that their words were not as important as their overall demeanor. Though they could not understand what was being said, Maggie could. The kids were having the best time of their lives. They laughed and chattered, then hugged the older people and disappeared back into the dark cavity of the motorhome. The elderly couple laughed heartily as the motorhome once again began shaking. Maggie no longer blamed the motorhome for taking up her time. "Dad, maybe next time we should bring more family and take a motorhome," she said dreamily.

Father didn't respond. He was preoccupied with collecting the proper amount of cash for the entrance fee, as well as fetching his driver's license from its cramped little wedge on the inside fold of his wallet.

Maggie continued to look behind. She couldn't help but notice that the three vehicles behind her were each completely different from the other. She tried to imagine a scenario where all of these groups would be gathered together, "A concert? No. How about a movie or a restaurant, or baseball game? Unlikely." She could think of no other place. "Dad, I had no idea that so many different kinds of people would want to travel so far just to see the park. This place must be pretty dang special." said Maggie dreamily.

"Welcome to the Rim Entrance of Grand Smoky Yellowsemite National Park," interrupted a sweet female voice coming from her father's open window. Maggie turned all her attention to the person outside.

"Hi!" blurted Maggie.

The woman on the outside lowered herself so that she could make eye contact with Maggie. She wore a wide brimmed hat made of rigid felt. As she got level with Maggie she raised the brim of her hat so the two could see each other. The woman was dressed in a freshly pressed uniform colored in earth tones, greens and browns. She had a small black, metallic, rectangular name badge pinned to her left breast pocket. Her name was sharply etched in gold upon the black matte, but Maggie had no desire to read it. She only locked eyes with the ranger.

Maggie was overcome with emotion. She had waited, for what seemed like, an eternity to be here. She had driven so long that she didn't know if her legs worked anymore. Maggie and her father had traveled across vast farmland, triumphed the ever climbing plateau, trudged across the land of hills and reservoirs, and survived the vast expanse of the flat cotton flinging desert. She had been haunted by a book and bewildered by a rickety old man. She had even seen a side of her father that she did not know existed. She had never expected to experience so many new things in such as a short amount of time. And now, she and her father were at the doorstep of their destination, being welcomed warmly by a park steward. Maggie couldn't think to say anything. Surely she had a hundred questions to ask about the weather forecast, or what trails were closed, or where the large game animals were foraging, but all she could do was smile back at the ranger.

Father handed the ranger a folded bill to pay the entrance fee. The ranger took the money and disappeared briefly. She returned and taped a printed receipt to the inside of the windshield. Then the ranger handed Father a small stack of folded pamphlets. Father, without looking, handed them directly to Maggie. Maggie set them on her lap and looked at the trove of information she had just acquired.

"Your pass is good for one week. Enjoy your stay!" exclaimed the ranger.

And with that Father, engaged the car into gear and rolled slowly away from the wooden hut. There was a brief stillness before Maggie registered what had just occurred. Her stomach tightened in triumphant excitement. She was now inside the park. She felt like a player about to take her first swing in a Major League Baseball game. She blinked slowly and smiled in celebration of the accomplishment. But just as a batter must hit the ball, so must Maggie explore. She looked up and out in front of her.

"Oh my!" exclaimed Maggie, "It's beautiful." There, in front of the two travelers, from atop the hill, Yellowsemite Valley spread out in all directions before them.

"Wow! that's a view," chimed Father.

It was undeniably breathtaking. The entrance into the park allowed for an uninterrupted view for miles in all directions. The point they descended from, was actually the western rim of The Flat Grey Dirt Desert. The rim spread out broadly to the left and to the right and dropped steeply to the base of the valley. It resembled an enormous sand dune that arched in a continuous crescent. Separating the rim of the desert with Yellowsemite Valley was the grand and glorious Flowy River. The late afternoon sun made the river look a deep burgundy. A thousand small burning reflections of yellow sunlight flashed within its strong and steady current. Beyond the grassy banks of the river, Yellowsemite Valley extended out far into the horizon towards tall, craggy mountains to the southwest. More gently, less impenetrable mountains bordered the valley to the north. A slight haze hung below the highest of that range's peaks. It draped over the lower reaches like fine- silken mosquito netting, covering a southern estate house bed set.

Maggie sat at full attention as the car steadily dropped lower off of the desert dune and closer to the river. Her head darted in all directions, the way a deer might enter an open meadow in search of predators. She strained against the setting light to take in the scene. The valley seemed subdued in the intense, evening light. The mountain ranges cast long outstretched shadows into the valley. She looked far to the northern reach of the valley in hopes of seeing Yellowsemite Lake.

Johnny Muur had discovered the valley, very close to where Maggie and her father were now entering from. He had written extensively about the many unique features found in and around the lake such as; it's bizarre tufas and fumaroles, the geyser pupfish, the paradox frog and six foot long giant salamander. He had written that he could see its immensity, from the banks of the Flowy River, on which he had first stumbled on that fateful morning, many years ago. Maggie saw no sign of the lake in the ever darkening, evening light.

They reached the bottom of the dune and immediately drove across an old arching bridge over the Flowy River. The bridge was made entirely of smooth river stone and mortar. The stones covered the surface of the bridge like irregular shaped, glistening kernels on a cob of corn. The many bulging stones that comprised the road surface made the car shudder uncontrollably. The car clopped and thudded noisily across the bridge and made the occupants feel slightly uncomfortable, having not experienced any similar terrain in the many miles they had traveled thus far.

Maggie looked into the river as they crossed over it. Even in the fading light Maggie could see clearly into its depths. Large angular boulders bulged up from the bottom. Small angular, and even smaller rounded stones, were faintly visible on the riverbed well below. Maggie was excited and frightened at the same time looking into the water. She wanted to jump in the pristine water, and yet, something in the back of her mind warned of danger. She knew where the feeling came from. She shook it away with a shiver and a shake, and looked forward into the lush meadow that lay on the other side of the river bank. They crossed over the bridge into the meadow without breaking stride.

Broadleaves of parsnip, blades of iris, tear dropped umbels of bleeding heart, and every other manner of forb, met the edge of the road in unabashed hordes growing amongst thick and thriving, thigh high fountain grass. The air was heavy with pollen and moisture, and buzzing insects. Most of the wildflowers had closed up for the evening, choosing to slumber with the setting sun. A few remained open. These flowers were a pure white and glowed brightly in the fading light. Trumpet like in shape, they arched up and away from their host plant gracefully.

Something large and birdlike fluttered up and into a passing blossom in search of nectar. "Did you see that?" asked Maggie excitedly.

"The moth?" presumed Father.

"Is that what it was? It looked like a weird bird." Maggie's eyes were wide with wonder.

"Yeah I think it's called a hawk moth. Birds and bees aren't the only things that pollinate flowers. If we're lucky we might even get to see bats doing it. How do you think the stargazer lily tree gets pollinated?" Father answered.

"No way!" said Maggie in awe. She leaned forward up against the dashboard to better see the procession taking place outside of the cab.

More winged creatures dashed and darted across the road, desperately searching out their meals, before day's end. With the discovery of the alleged hawk moth, Maggie couldn't tell whether the creatures were birds, or moths, or possibly even bats.

"Umm Maggie?" asked Father inquiringly.

"Yeah Dad," replied Maggie dreamily.

"Can you open up that map and look up Yellowsemite lodge?" asked Father.

Maggie looked down at her lap in surprise. She had forgotten about the pamphlets. "Ohh, sure Dad, hang on a sec." She geared through the papers talking out loud as she searched, "Park rules and regulations, calendar of events, umm summer news release, become a member, ehh, here it is! Park map".

Maggie unfolded the map carefully and deliberately so as not to rip any creases. The glossy paper was firm and crisp, like a poster she might later hang on her bedroom wall when she returned home. She strained against the darkening light to make out the map. She looked up and saw that the sun had now dropped just below the lofty, gnarled peaks bordering the far side of the valley. Sharply, defined rays of sunlight stuck out and above her like spot lights at a main event.

"Wow!" said Maggie holding her breath in awe.

"Uh, Maggie? If you don't mind, I'd like to get us to the lodge safely," interrupted father.

"Oh, sorry, right," said Maggie looking back down. "Do you mind if I turn on my overhead light then? It's getting pretty dark."

"Sure," replied Father.

The cab became dimly illuminated. "That's better," said Maggie, as she analyzed the map. "Now let's see here," she mumbled to herself. "We came in through the… east entrance, ooh they call it the Rim Entrance, that's clever, and the lodge is near the south shore of Yellowsemite Lake, which is north of us, sooo… Here it is! Yellowsemite Lodge," sounded Maggie triumphantly.

"And how far away is it?" continued Father.

"Umm…Well it's 24 miles from the Rim Entrance to Geyser Loop Road, then another 16 to the lodge so, 40? Less than 40 miles Dad," said Maggie looking up smiling at her father. "I'm so excited!" she wiggled jovially in her seat.

CHAPTER

14

The sun was well below the horizon and it was now necessary for headlights. The sharp, impressive rays that cast out from the mountains had disappeared. Only a reddish, purple glow backlit the far away skyline. The valley had all but disappeared. The only evidence of its presence was the lush growth of flora popping out from the edge of the road. Maggie looked ahead eagerly awaiting to catch sight of the lodge. It was over one hundred years old and made entirely out of timber. Maggie had seen photos of it when she had researched 'accommodations' on the internet at home. It was undeniably grand and impressive. Built in the same manner as a log cabin, but it looked more like a four-story, A-framed, mountain resort. Maggie was giddy at the notion of seeing the lodge in real life.

It had some very iconic features that Maggie recalled reading about. For instance, it was powered only by summer lightning storms. Apparently, there was a large lightning rod that stood far above the apex of the lodge. The rod traveled all the way from above the roof down below the ground-floor and was connected to enormous underground batteries. Every time lightning struck the rod, electricity was stored in the batteries.

The lodge also had famous works of art. One statue, in particular, intrigued Maggie. "What did it say?" pondered Maggie. "*Made by the original inhabitants of Yellowsemite. It now resides in front of the lodge. Presented as a peace offering when Johnny Muur rescued the chief's daughter during a* catastrophic wildfire. No one knows how old it is. Made entirely of black and red obsidian, and fashioned into a fearsome beast of ancient times."

And then there was the elevator, made from one single trunk of an ancient pine tree. Maggie couldn't remember all the details. Only that the online photos made it look really cool.

As the car drew nearer to the lodge, they entered a forested section. A large yellow sign on the side of the road read, "Black Forest- Turn lights on at all times." And with that, the travelers entered in.

All ambient light vanished, only the car's own headlights illuminated the way. Maggie couldn't help but feel a little spooked, by the tall pine trees lining the road. Their trunks were quite girthy, with thick gnarled bark covering the trees. Only the lowest branches were visible in the cloaked darkness. All of the branches were dead, not a needle to be found on them. No bark remained on the branches for protection, not even moss or lichen hung from a twig. Only smooth, white wood twisted and gnarled out in all directions, like the arms of a maddened sorcerer casting out an enchantment. Nothing grew on the forest floor. The only evidence of life at all was a thick, rust colored blanket of fallen pine needles. Maggie pressed her face against the cold passenger window and careened her neck skyward to try to get a glimpse of something, anything that might reveal an ounce of diversity in this wooded realm. She could not see the silhouette of skyline poking through the canopy. No hint of yellow moon glowing through the needles.

"This place is dark," admitted Maggie.

"It's black," chimed Father.

"Phuhh," Maggie exhaled in agreement. "It's so weird though. A minute ago, we were driving through a meadow with more kinds of wildflowers than I've seen in my whole life, and now, there's nothing. Nothing but these big scary trees," said Maggie in awe.

Father listened intently to his daughter's observations. He thumped his fingers rhythmically on the steering wheel as he tried to come up with an explanation. "Well," he said at last, "that's the thing about nature. It does whatever it's capable of."

Maggie looked at her father from the corner of her eyes skeptically. Her lips pressed firmly in agreement. "Whatever it's capable of?" she mocked.

Father was unperturbed. "Let's use this place as an example," he continued. "You said there are all kinds of wildflowers in the meadow right?"

Maggie nodded affirmingly.

"Well," he went on, "those wildflowers don't get very big, most of them are only waist high. So they probably don't have very deep roots growing into the soil. I bet if you took a shovel out there and started digging, it wouldn't take very long before you hit rock. I mean solid rock, or something so harsh that roots can't grow in it." He paused so Maggie could think about it. "Now look at these trees," he went on, "their trunks are absolutely massive. There is no way these trees have shallow root systems. Look!" he motioned. "Look at that one!" He pointed to a tree that had toppled over. It was stripped bare of bark, even on its trunk. Its smooth white wood looked ghostly against a blackened backdrop. "Look at those roots," he pointed. "They're massive."

He was correct. Several main roots had been ripped out of the ground when the tree had fallen. The largest of the roots were as big around as the tires of a semi-truck and projected out ten feet into the air.

"Ohh," exclaimed Maggie.

Father was not finished, "Those roots are broken off. They go even deeper into the ground. That means the soil must be very deep here. With that small amount of information we might be able to explain why the meadow has flowers, and why the forest is, well, forested." Father looked up ahead into the road. Maggie could see he was smirking confidently.

Maggie was impressed by her father's reasoning, but she was not satisfied. "Okay Dad," she retorted, "I understand why the trees are tall, but
why doesn't anything grow underneath the trees? I thought forests were
alive, not cemeteries for dead trees."

Father was prepared to match wits with his daughter. "That's easy Maggie," he answered boastfully, "plants need more than just soil and water
to survive. They need sunlight too. I don't think it's an accident that this
place is called The Black Forest. The pine trees above us are massive.
Their thick canopy of needles block out any light from above. I know it
sounds impossible, but that's it." Father looked down at Maggie with a
smile that suggested he knew he had won the battle of intellects.

"Daad," lectured Maggie.

"What?" responded Father innocently.

"Are we a little proud of ourselves?" chided Maggie. "Look at Dad," she
teased "the big scientist, got my plant knowledge on. Teaching the
youth," she laughed heartily.

Father was not moved. He was not about to have his moment of victory
spoiled so easily. "Well Mags, your Pop's knows what he knows," he said
confidently, still smirking at his wisdom.

Maggie smiled up at her father adoringly. He was her rock. He always
had been. As she gazed at him, she thought about how thankful she was
to have him as a father, regardless of the recent struggles they had gone
through. Something twinkled far out in the blackness behind him. Maggie focused on the point she thought it had came from. It twinkled again.

"Dad, I see something," declared Maggie.

"We should almost be at the lodge by now," presumed Father. "Ahh," he
exclaimed, "here we go."

Up ahead was a rectangular green park sign. Dense foliage covered the ground beneath the sign. The car's headlights shown a little farther out past the sign.

"It's a clearing," remarked Maggie.

The car traveled closer to the sign though its words were not quite visible. Maggie could see the forest's edge. She could see stars glistening far out in the distance. She was relieved that she did not have to bear the bleakness of The Black Forest any longer. She dreaded the thought of getting lost in such a place.

"Yellowsemite Lodge ½ mile to the left," said Father resolutely as they passed the sign.

The forest cleared and a plethora of wildflowers welcomed them out of the darkness. Father flipped on his turn signal and slowed the car to make the turn. Maggie couldn't see the lodge because the road followed along the edge of the forest. She could, however, see a yellow glow above the treeline a short distance ahead. Perhaps it was the lodge.

The road traveled a short distance along the forest edge and then opened up on all sides into what appeared, to Maggie, to be a large, somewhat round clearing. There at the far end of the expanse was the lodge. Bright floodlights cast far out into the open space, sending out soft beams of visibility into the dark meadow. The grand structure was well lit. Even from across the clearing, the building impressed upon Maggie. It's steeply pitched roof pointed up darkly into the starlit night. From its apex, erected the large lightning rod that towered skyward. Floodlights pointed up to its tip. From the tip hung a large flag. There was no breeze to billow the flag so Maggie could not see what was embossed upon its royal blue, stitched fabric. There was no lighting pointed directly at the lodge itself, so as to not disturb the occupants inside. There was enough ambient light to see countless windows dotting all levels of the lodge. Some were lit, some were not. Some with shades drawn, and some had their windows open. Maggie couldn't wait to look out from one.

As their car drew closer, she could see a large open deck, above what looked to be the main entrance. The tops of people's heads were back lit and stuck out above the balcony. A large fire blazed upon the deck sending burning, swirling embers into the fresh mountain air. Shadows of people standing, stretched out upon the slanted shingle roof behind them. The shadows swayed rhythmically as if entranced by some chant or folk song. It was a very peaceful setting.

Father drove the car right up to the lodge entrance. The drive to it made a large roundabout, so that all traffic traveled in one direction from right to left. In the center of the roundabout was a simple lawn with small flood lights pointing towards its center. In the center was a large and impressive statue of a bear. The bear statue was made out of a hard stone that reflected magnificently in the lighting. The stone was a deep black composition with flecks of maroon interspersed. Each maker's mark etched sharply as if chipped away. Maggie stared at the statue as they rounded it. Each chip mark's edge glimmered brightly and light danced downward as Maggie's viewpoint changed. There were thousands of chip marks on the bear statue and each chip reflected in its own light. The bear looked as if it was raining small, bright yellow drops on its dark hide. The sight caught Maggie completely off guard. Not only was its design striking, but so too was the object itself. Maggie had never seen a bear like it before. She had read up thoroughly on the park's wildlife. She knew there were two species of bear in the park, brown bear and black bear, but this bear was neither.

This specimen stood taller from the ground. It's paws were the size of hubcaps. Long jagged claws reached out several inches further. It's build was stronger and less cumbersome. And it's face... it's face was most intriguing of all. Instead of having a long shepherd like snout, its nose was blunt, like a pit bull. Four large incisors struck out from its mouth like sharp glistening daggers. Maggie was slightly horrified as she contemplated the chance encounter with such a beast.

Father parked the car with the slightest squeak of its brakes. A young man with an oversized peaked cap covering an overgrown curly mop of hair walked quickly over to them. The boy of a man walked around to Father's window and waited patiently beside the door. Father rolled down the window. The boy spoke, "Welcome to Yellowsemite Lodge. Will you be staying the night?"

"We will," replied Father.

"Your name sir?" asked the boy.

"Mursen, the reservation is under Mursen," replied Father

"Mursen, yes we've been expecting you," responded the boy in the cumbersome looking peaked cap. The boy signaled back to a group of other valets who quickly rolled some empty carts over. Father opened the trunk and the car began to get unloaded.

"Anything that needs to stay in the car sir?" replied a young girl.

"We'll only need our suitcases and sleeping items and ice chest brought in. Thank you," answered Father with a smile and nod.

The boy with the oversized peaked cap spoke again, "Well if there isn't anything else sir, we will get your things brought to your room promptly. If you would like, valet services can park your car for you while you get your reservations in order?" Father silently nodded that was his intention. The boy continued, "In that case, please leave your car key with the receptionist at the kiosk over there, and then check in with concierge. It will be the large desk, straight ahead inside."

"Thank you," replied Father and started shuffling out of the car. Maggie, realizing that it was time to get out, quickly surveyed around the cab to collect any and all articles that had been used and left out of place during the day's confined escapades. Maggie stuffed her belongings into her backpack and stepped out into the cool, yet slightly balmy air.

Father was already walking towards the valet. He didn't even look back to see if Maggie was following. Maggie flung her backpack over one shoulder and scampered after him.

"Have fun!" said the boy.

Maggie looked back without losing any momentum. "Thank you," she said shakingly. She caught up to Father at the valet kiosk.

Father glanced at Maggie as he handed the valet his keys. "Maggie," he murmured, "I was beginning to think you were going to sleep in the car for another night."

Maggie laughed hesitantly. He hadn't commented once as to how much driving was required to get to this place, but he must have been anxious to get out of the car. And seeing how quickly he got out confirmed Maggie's suspicions. He handed his car key to the receptionist and, without so much as a pause, walked briskly up a wide flight of shiny, stone steps towards the main door. Maggie scurried quickly behind him to keep up the pace.

They entered into the lobby. It was charming and rugged. Round logs made the walls. The floor and ceiling were panelled timber. The room had enough space to house a couple of couches and a rock mantled fireplace. Large oil paintings of mountain landscapes hung about. Their thick wooden frames were nearly as magnificent as the paintings. Father strided straight to the front desk.

"Hello," said a woman's voice from behind the counter.

"Hello," replied Father, "Mursen checking in."

"One moment please," said the woman's voice softly, shuffling a couple of papers, "here we go sir." She handed Father the usual forms to sign regarding billing, car information, and insurance. He began reviewing the paperwork and handed the receptionist his credit card in return. The lady continued, "Unfortunately the dining room is now closed, but you can order room service. A menu is in your room. Breakfast is served in the Sunrise Cafe, that's on the east wing of the lodge. Food is served between six and ten. Lunch is served between ten and three, that's on the second floor directly above us in the the Timber Diner. Dinner is served most nights from five to nine. And that'll be at Muur's End which is just this way (motioning with her arm to the left)."

"That's our name!" exclaimed Maggie.

The woman stopped talking and looked at Maggie blankly. She looked down at Father's credit card and chuckled ever so slightly, "Almost dear, Muur's End," she enunciated clearly and slowly, "not Mursen".

"Oh," remarked Maggie sheepishly. She smiled sincerely with flushed cheeks.

The receptionist quickly resumed her obligatory talking points before Maggie could interject any further, "Room service is served twenty four hours a day, seven days a week. Dial two on your room phone. Front desk is zero. Park channel on the TV is channel one and TV Guide is zero. Here's your card sir. Will there be anything else this evening?"

Father was looking down to sign the final document, "No that's fine, thank you," he responded without looking up.

"How many room keys sir?" the attendant asked.

"One should be fine," he responded quickly handing the attendant the final papers. He looked at Maggie and paused to think. "You know what, I'll take two keys," he said to the attendant without taking his eyes off of Maggie.

"Here you go, enjoy your stay," replied the woman, "your room is on the fourth floor. The elevator is here to your right. Your room will be on the left."

"Thank you," said Father as he stepped towards the elevator.

"Thank you," parroted Maggie as she scurried awkwardly to keep pace with her father.

Maggie shuffled in front of her father to the elevator. It was easy to find as two large, wooden doors bulged out into the room in a pronounced circular fashion. She pushed the button eagerly. There was a muffled echo of metal and cable that emanated from the other side of the door, followed by a brief pause, then the doors opened. The inside of the elevator was well lit. It was made entirely of wood and perfectly circular.

"Awesome," whispered Maggie excitedly.

Maggie and her father stepped inside. Maggie took a deep breath and exhaled peacefully. Her olfactory was overloaded by the smell of the wood. The aroma was crisp and strong with hints of vanilla, nutmeg and pepper. Any tension she carried with her quickly dissolved away inside of the fragrant wooden cylinder. Father pressed the button for the fourth floor. The two stood in silence as they ascended up into the lodge.

Maggie inspected the elevator walls as the large doors sealed silently. The craftwork of the elevator was so well done that the doors almost vanished into the tapestry of the surrounding wood once they had sealed. She had never been inside of such a unique elevator. The wood was undeniably old given the maze like patchwork of tunnels that had been burrowed out of the facia, the work of termites and grubs. Some sections had clusters of holes where the insects had wrought havoc. Other sections were devoid, showing only virgin timber.

Maggie noticed one bore that was larger than the rest. As she peered closer to it, Maggie felt inside the groove of the hole, which was surprisingly not round at all. It had distinct edges that spiraled, equal distances around each other. Maggie followed the bore with her finger. She was so mystified by the hole that she didn't even hear the "ding" of the elevator, signaling that they had reached the third floor.

"Maggie," alerted Father.

Maggie turned around quickly, "Yes Dad?" Her face looked utterly curious as to why he had broken her train of thought.

Father looked at her with incredulity. He tried to mask it, but he was tired of driving, and excited to be in the park at long last. The only thing he wanted was to rest for the night, and explore the park in the morning. He held his breath trying not to speak harshly to Maggie, hoping she would figure out that it was time to simply get out of the elevator.

At last he spoke flatly, "Um… we're on the fourth floor."

Maggie looked behind him to the hallway, "Oh!" she said, "Right."

Walking out of the elevator, Maggie was still spellbound by the large hole she had discovered. She could see the boring, when she looked behind her as she crossed out into the hallway. It traveled along the wall in a gradually ascending fashion almost like an enormous, graceful spiral. Father began walking determinedly down the hall. His footsteps clapped on the hardwood floors quietly. Maggie followed the hole as the elevator doors closed. She couldn't tell from where she was standing but it looked as though the hole traveled all the way around the room. Father's footsteps were barely audible. He had already turned the corner. She scampered quickly after him. As she reached the corner she took one more look back at the elevator. It's rounded doors bulged out into the hallway, like a man with tight pants and an overhanging pot belly. Father was stepping into their room as she rounded the corner. She hurried and followed him inside.

CHAPTER

16

I t was cold outside and the wind blew faintly over thick folded blades of robust green grass. The lush field stretched far away, until out of sight. A dark cloud mass, threatening rain, hovered low to the ground, in the not so far off distance. The mass spun slowly and outstretched wispy tendrils of vapor up in front of it like an octopus traveling over the seafloor. The sky had a backlit purple tinge to it. The sun was nowhere to be found.

A dark spot moved from beneath the cloud mass. At first the spot was so far away, it was indiscernible. As the object moved closer, it became more defined. It was a person, running. Running wildly away from the storm. As the person came nearer his features became visible. It was a man. His gate was heavy and almost mechanical as he ran over the large clumps of waist high grass. His clothes were ragged and bleached from the sun, sweat, and dirt. His arms flew out high in front of him to keep his balance as he hurdled clumps and avoided pitfalls. Thunder rumbled inside the looming storm.

The man's face took definition. He was an older man and his face was charred from years of weathering. He bore a scraggly, grey beard that pressed against his chest as he lumbered across the field. He looked scared. It was Johnny.

His breath was heavy and labored, air squeaking in and out of his throat like a broken accordion. His footsteps thudded and crunched haphazardly closer, while his lungs sucked in air as best they could. Thunder rumbled louder and closer. Fat drops of rain began to pat against thick blades of grass.

His eyes were wide with fear and looked out into nothing. Mouth agape, he wanted to shriek but was unable to, due to the relentless exertion of flight. He drew ever closer, as did the storm. The low hanging cloudmass devoured the landscape in a violent swirling darkness. Wind escaped from underneath the cloud mass and blew ever harder. The rain fell stronger.

Johnny was saturated from the water that sheeted off of him. He stumbled and flew forward landing hard upon his stomach. His body convulsed with each desperate breath for air. His breath was rapid and clamorous. With his face buried in the grass, he outstretched one arm weakly. It shook wearily from exhaustion. He grabbed a stalk of grass near to him and pushed away from it, which helped him to roll over. This arduous task, made him groan painfully. Water fountained off his prostrate body and flowed over, to the ground beneath him. Staring up into the dark sky above him, his pupils became dilated into two black orbs. His chest heaved forcefully to take in oxygen. Johnny was losing strength.

The rain now fell steadily, saturating the ground and grass all around. Rain splattered into an incessant drum roll like a thousand pairs of small hands applauding. Johnny's torso no longer heaved. His mouth fell open and hung loosely, while his body quivered and shook faintly. His black eyes were glossy and lifeless, staring up into a stormy heaven.

The sky darkened and the rain soaked the earth with relentless abandon. Standing water that had puddled moments ago, was now deepening. Johnny's lifeless body began to be buried in water. What was once a tall field of sturdy grass was now becoming a shallow sea.

The water rose to his ears, then to his mouth. Eventually, it reached his eyes and Johnny did not resist. The water continued to rise until even the tallest blades of grass were submerged in clear rain water. Johnny's body could be seen at the bottom and still the rain did not cease. The water rose higher, until the body was just a blurry object amongst the green.

Suddenly, the object moved. It thrashed about violently, to the left and to the right, viciously, as if trying to free itself from a stranglehold. The object stopped and then began to gain definition. Johnny was rising to the surface quickly. He shot out to of the water like a rising rocket. Life was once again in his eyes. He had a half crazed look upon his face as though he had just discovered a motherlode of placer.

As he lost momentum, and began falling back down to the water he screamed one thing, "Freeeeeeeeeeee!!!!!!!!!!!"

Maggie awoke to a risen sun, in a room she had fallen asleep in the night before. The room's single window was cracked open allowing a vociferous meadowlark to rouse Maggie into an awakened state.

Maggie's bed sheets were drenched in sweat, making her feel very uncomfortable. She sat up in her bed and recalculated what had just occurred. Her heart pounded as though she had been the one running from the storm. She strained to fight the urge to panic.

"Was I dreaming?" she thought to herself, "Why is he back in my dreams?" She looked at the adjoining bed expecting to find her father. Instead, the only signs of his presence, were his reading glasses on the bedside table and an unmade bed. She listened for him in the bathroom. Nothing.

"Uhh," she groaned aloud, "why is he acting this way? As soon as we got here he hasn't said one thing to me. And now he's left me. Uhh," she groaned again.

Maggie got out of bed and made her way to the bathroom pressing her fingers against her forehead as if trying to soothe a headache. She went to the sink, poured herself a glass of water, feverishly drank from it and looked into the mirror. She looked normal, but she didn't feel normal. The dream she had just awoken from was way too similar to the vision she had days prior when she had first started out on her journey. And her father was not acting normal either. He was always a quiet man, and very calculated, but he would never take off without telling Maggie.

"What is going on with him?" groaned Maggie. She walked out of the bathroom and glanced at the door. A note had been left on the door knob. Maggie quickly snatched it up and began reading, "Good morning sunshine. I'm down at the Sunrise Cafe (East Wing). Hurry up. We have a big day ahead of us." And with that, Maggie smiled wide. She was relieved to know her father was still very much aware of her existence. Maggie then rushed about, changing into clothes for the day.

The Sunrise Cafe was easy to find although it was more of a cafeteria than a cafe. Hordes of people crammed every sitting space available. Of course Maggie showed up during the morning commute. The cafe was a large dining hall with an open beam ceiling and wall to wall windows lining the left and right side. A self-serve buffet lined the far wall. And a long bulletin board decorated the wall from which she had entered.

The room was noisy. Voices of all pitches, ages, and languages squawked constantly. Silverware clanked, papers rustled and kids skirted in and out of sight. Having finished their breakfast, the parents dismissed their kids, so they could plan for the day's activities. "But where is Dad?" thought Maggie. Her stomach growled in protest, wanting to eat first and do the searching second.

"This was a terrible idea," she said aloud in a stressful tone, realizing that his cute note on the door was no longer cute. Maggie surveyed the room. There were people everywhere. Her stomach growled again. "Forget it," she said adamantly, "I'm eating. He can find me." She crossed her arms stiffly and marched to the other side of the cafeteria, joining a small line of patrons waiting to fill their plates. Maggie searched the hall as she waited. No sign of him anywhere.

Somebody closed a door behind her and Maggie spun around to investigate. She hadn't noticed when she first walked over, but there were two glass french doors that led out to a very pleasant stamped, concrete patio. Several round tables were set up for dining. The patio overlooked the entrance to the lodge and surrounding meadow. "That looks like a nice place to eat," she thought.

Maggie filled her plate with an assortment of steaming ostrich eggs, caribou sausage and squirrel bacon, as well as chanterelle mushroom yogurt, marble rye toast and gooseberry jelly. With an overfilled plate, she thought it best to come back for a drink later. She decided to give up looking for her father and instead fill her belly. "He can try to find me for once," she said with a hint of scorn.

Maggie softly stepped her way towards the french doors, deftly avoiding the pandemonium of the packed cafeteria. She balanced her meal delicately so as not to lose one morsel, turned the polished handle, and stepped outside.

She felt instantly better having done so. The morning air felt crisp and cool. A sunlit window behind her radiated heat on her back, which felt good. She smiled discreetly and closed the door behind her. The raucous noise inside instantly muted. A few songbirds chirped in the, not so far off, forest to her right. The songbirds perfectly replaced the giddy screams of unsupervised children on the other side of the clear glass windows.

The people eating on the patio were much quieter, opting to do more listening than speaking. Maggie searched for a place to sit. She saw a couple of open places scattered around the patio. She noticed one towards the back, up against one of the cafeteria windows.

"That's a good spot," she thought, "Dad can see me from inside at the entrance and I can see him if comes out here."

Maggie walked over carefully with both hands holding her plate. She slid her chair out with a concerted sweep from her leg and sat down. She let out a triumphant sigh and started cutting away at the caribou sausage. Oily juices popped out of the steaming meat and ran over the base of her overloaded plate. She stabbed at a juicy morsel and took a bite. As she chewed, a whirlwind of thoughts ran through her mind.

"Where is my Dad?" she thought. "He is not acting like his normal self. He is so distant all of a sudden. And what are we going to do today?" Maggie grabbed another piece of sausage. She chewed with dedicated fervor as she contemplated this thought.

"I should be excited," she thought, "I've never been so excited to be somewhere before. I've never seen such a beautiful place... but I'm kind of scared." Maggie put down her fork and picked up a spoon. She began eating her chanterelle yogurt. It was creamy, golden yellow color and quite delicious.

"Why did I have another dream last night?" She furrowed her brow in deep contemplation, unaware that a small group of three, well dressed, individuals had sat down at an empty table near her, which happened to be the farthest table on the patio. They all had very somber looks on their faces. All were in deep contemplation, just like Maggie.

The three individuals sat down silently, removed the "reserved" placard that had been stationed at the center of their table, and remained silent. Maggie was unaware to what was transpiring around her.

"He was in my dream again," thought Maggie, "I watched him die. It was terrifying." She grabbed a piece of toast to eat.

"Why do I keep getting haunted?" she thought, "I can't deal with this. I just want to have a fun adventure in the park with my dad, but I can't because he's not even here with me." Maggie set down her toast defeatedly. She rested her elbows on the table, ran her fingers deep into her scalp and looked down longingly at her food. She had lost her appetite. She had never felt so out of place in her life.

A chair nearby squeaked to her left and Maggie's concentration was broken. She keyed in on the table beside her, without making it obvious that she was eavesdropping. A woman came and joined the table that the three men had sat at. Every person at that table was dressed professionally and did not look like tourists. The men waited silently and watched the woman intently, while she got settled. Maggie spied her discretely. She wore a straw cowboy hat and had a tightly tied ponytail of blonde hair running down passed her shoulder. She wore clothing similar to the park uniform like the ranger at the Rim Entrance had worn. She wore ankle high hiking boots that were well worn and also quite muddy.

"Good morning gentleman," said the woman quietly.

"Good morning Dr. Andrews," the men said in near unison.

"How is the child?" asked the doctor firmly.

One of the men leaned back in his chair and subconsciously wiped something from below his breast pocket. He spoke hesitantly, "The child is stable. He sustained minor lacerations to his legs... we're guessing from running...a few bruises to his ribs, where he must have fallen while running." The man paused to collect himself, "The injuries to his right arm are severe... tissue tearing in several places as though it was ripped apart... and multiple fractures to the humerus..." the group looked away in discomfort. The man continued, "The surgeon is confident that all of these wounds can heal...it's the head injuries that we are monitoring. The boy has several points on his skull that appear to be pierced... or punctured. The surgeon agrees with your initial observations and believes these injuries indicate bite marks."

The group once again became squeamish upon hearing the news. The man continued, "He is still unconscious. They have stopped the bleeding, but we don't know what his state will be like when he becomes conscious... if he becomes conscious."

Maggie was wide eyed. She did not want to hear such a gruesome story, nor could she distract herself from it. She reached for a piece of toast and forced herself to eat it so as not to alert the group of her listening in.

The group continued their discussion unbeknownst to Maggie's presence. One of the other men, who was older and adorned a heavy gold watch, spoke next, "I don't understand it Jim. Mammoths have never even shown aggression to people. You could ride one if the park rules allowed it. How could one do this to the boy?"

"This was not done by a mammoth sir," spoke the last of the three men. He was the youngest of the group and was dressed in something similar to a park uniform. He wore leather cowboy boots that had a little mud clustered up along the sole. "When I discovered the boy in my patrol car, I noticed a group of mammoths huddled in a protective circle. I assumed that wolves or possibly even one of the sabertooths had tried at one of their yearlings. I stopped and observed the group. Once the group spotted me they moved off into the forest, leaving the boy behind. That's when I radioed for the medivac."

The man with the heavy gold watch spoke again. "So you're saying a sabertooth did this?" his tone was a little louder and somewhat incredulous. Jim placed his hand on the older man so as to calm him.

"Sabers don't behave like this either Art," said Jim reinforcing, "plus they stay in the high country. Even the tagged ones don't come down lower than six thousand feet. They go after the big horns and markhors and marmots. In our two hundred years of operation, we've never even heard of an interaction of this nature with people."

Art looked at the three others pleadingly, "Then what?" with tension in his voice, "A boy has nearly died in my my park and you're telling me that wolves did it?" He looked around at the three others as though he dared them to make the argument.

Maggie swallowed the last of her toast. Her mouth was parched and she wished she had gotten something to drink before she tuned in on the conversation. She grabbed a piece of bacon and pretended to enjoy eating it, although she desperately needed a refreshment.

Art turned to the woman, "Dr. Andrews, this is your area of expertise. What have you got?"

Maggie couldn't see the doctor's face as she was positioned facing the same direction as Maggie. She could barely make out what the doctor was saying.

"No sir, this attack was not from wolves either, although there is strong evidence to infer that this was done by a predator" explained the doctor. "The injuries on his arm suggest that the animal had a paw roughly twelve inches in diameter, or the size of a large baseball glove, skull injuries suggest bite marks from a jaw with the crushing power equal to that of an alligator."

Art nearly thrust out of his seat in protest, but quickly subdued his actions so as not to rouse the attention of anyone within listening distance. "There is no predator in the world today, that is that big and powerful," he interrupted.

"That is correct sir, or at least we thought that was correct," she paused awkwardly and looked out past the patio, towards the lodge entrance. The men and Maggie turned with her to see what she was looking at. The only thing they could be looking at was the statue of the enormous bear.

"Impossible," said Jim returning his attention back to the group, "can't be." He shook his head in disbelief, "The short faced bear has been extinct for 5000 years. Even the local tribes believe they're extinct."

Dr Andrews went on, ignoring Jim's denial, "I was able to do a thorough field study last night until about 8 o'clock this morning. I reconstructed the incident by measuring the distance between footprints, paw prints, hoof prints, blood, and saliva samples. My data points are entered into the CAD program on my laptop. I encourage all of you to look at them... Here are the facts. The boy spotted the bear and ran in the opposite direction. They were separated by about nearly a mile. The bear took chase. I don't know why but the boy ran towards the mammoths, which is certainly the reason why he survived the attack. The bear caught up with him before he reached the herd. The herd defended the boy the same way they defend a stranded calf, by charging as a wall. The bear had the boy pinned down but fled once the mammoths encroached to within three meters. The boy never moved from the point of the attack, suggesting he was already unconscious. The mammoths circled around the boy for about an hour until Captain Sperry found the herd, which puts the time of attack at around 6pm. The entire attack, from the moment of encounter until the bear fled, lasted only about two minutes. We are running DNA samples in the lab and cross referencing our results with the University database. We won't know for sure until our results are confirmed, but the saliva and hair samples taken near the boy's injuries are definitely ursidae, or in the bear family, but not grizzly bear, nor polar bear, which is of course very unlikely." Andrews fell silent.

The men stared at her in confusion, all desperately seeking to understand why she believed that an enormous, extinct bear was the culprit.

"But why?" implored Art. "Why do you believe it's a short faced?"

The doctor continued with her observations, "The distance between forepaws and hind paws, when the bear was not running, are nearly six feet apart, the largest grizzlies are only about four and a half feet apart. Paw depressions in the soil suggest the animal weighed about two thousand pounds, the average grizzly weighs less than half of that. The largest recorded grizzlies are up in Aleutia 8000 miles from here and don't even come close to the size that my research is pointing towards. The largest bears we've encountered in the park still fall short by about eight hundred pounds. Once the bear began running, assuming the boy ran fifteen miles an hour, the bear sustained a speed of, at least thirty miles an hour." She looked around at her stunned audience and continued hesitantly, "When you factor in the destruction, the boy's arm, which is from only one swipe from the claw, and teeth marks from his skull, there are no other predators that fit the profile." The group fell silent.

Jim spread out his arms in front of him and stammered out in defense, "We're talking about an animal that went extinct during the last ice age. How, with all of our discoveries, could we have missed this?"

Dr Andrews rebutted calmly, "Much of the plains to the north of the Smoky Range are still unexplored. Bison frequently migrate from there down to Yellowsemite Valley in the winter. The short faced bear's main prey was the bison. Theoretically, there has been strong enough bison populations to sustain a small population of the short faced to present day. If this is true, then it is possible that a bear could follow the herd into the park. Gentlemen" the doctor paused to collect her next words, "I know this information sounds unbelievable but this is where my preliminary observations have led. For the sake of the security of the people in this park, I hope I am wrong, but I strongly urge this group to prepare to encounter a creature of this magnitude."

Art looked at Dr. Andrews. It was obvious that he had something to say but he was trying figure out how to say it correctly. At last he spoke, "Doctor, you are one of the most distinguished field biologists this park has ever had on staff. You have many achievements and discoveries that you have made throughout your career (he paused, biting his lip) but I can't go out and tell the world that a long extinct animal has suddenly re-emerged in the park and is running around attacking innocent children." He paused again and looked firmly at the center of the table. "Now I'm grateful that the three of you met me on such short notice but perhaps we should not have had this meeting in such a public place." Their eyes darted about the patio to see if anyone had taken notice of them. Maggie was already chewing on her last piece of bacon. She anticipated them looking around and tried to look as ignorant as she could, which made her feel very foolish.

Art continued, "So here's what we're going to do. Jim, you keep in contact with the family. Do everything you can to help them. I don't want them to even consider reaching out to the media. Tell them it was a bear, a big bear. Dr. Andrews, where is this animal now?"

"The bear fled in the same direction from where it had come from, to the west, towards The Roaring River. I left my two best trackers at the site to continue to search for the animal." responded Dr. Andrews.

"Okay, that's not so bad. We don't have any campgrounds in that area for ten miles. What kind of search radius are we looking at?" asked Art.

Dr. Andrews paused for a moment to calculate, "Well, given the animal's propensity for flat land and ability to move quickly...80 miles?"

"80 miles?" repeated Art in disbelief, "that's a quarter of the park."

"Well sir, we simply don't know enough about the animal's habits to reach a smaller estimate," said the doctor.

Art sighed deeply and looked back at the center of the table. "Alright," he said in submission. "Captain Sperry, pull out your notepad. First thing, I want the entire ranger staff running nine hour shifts in three different groups; morning, swing, and graveyard. Have reception call in all seasonal staff. Put the least experienced staff on vehicle watch with an animal specialist, one to one ratio. Nobody, and I mean nobody, works alone. Place the most experienced staff to monitor campgrounds and any other area that has high traffic, shopping centers, hotels, and major attractions. If anyone wants to know, we are monitoring for POSSIBLE increased geothermal activity. Second thing, this is a tranquilize and capture scenario. I want four capture teams stationed at key intersections 'round the clock." turning to Dr. Andrews, "If this thing is as big as you say it is, use enough tranquilizer to set a mammoth right on its butt. If this thing truly does exist, it may be wise to keep it alive. Only use deadly force if absolutely necessary. Third," turning to Jim "link up with the Forestry Service. I want every helicopter they can spare up in the air, looking for this thing. If they've got thermal scanners and can fly at night, I'm okay with that. I'll divert all air traffic to the west gate airfield. They are instructed to search out, report and track any predator over 300 lbs. Dr Andrews, you are side by side with Sperry. If he knows about it, you know about it. We are going to find this thing before sundown. Photograph whatever is necessary. And most important, I want hourly updates from each of you. We are not going to let another person get attacked by this... whatever it is." He slammed his fist on the table vehemently. Art stared around the table and looked deeply at his audience, "Good luck to us all."

And with that, the officials got out of their seats quietly, and briskly walked away to tend to their tasks.

Maggie was mortified. She had just overheard the most chilling conversation imaginable. She stared off into the meadow and then at the menacing statue of red and black obsidian. She imagined stumbling upon a massive bear while out hiking and shivered at the thought.

"Margaret Mursen!" scolded a very familiar voice.

Maggie, still shocked from what she had just overheard, turned her attention groggily to the voice.

"Where have you been all morning?" demanded her father, "I've been looking for you everywhere."

Maggie came out of her daze and suddenly felt all of her previous emotions re-emerge. "Where have I been?" she asked rhetorically. "Where have YOU been?" she accused.

Father stood over Maggie, hunched forward in an intimidating kind of way. "Where have I been?" he balked, "I've spent the last two hours waiting in that cafe for you. That's where I've been."

Maggie was not going to be intimidated so easily, "In that little cafe huh? Well there's like a hundred and fifty people in that little cafe and I looked for you. I did, but I was starving, and I was nervous, cause I was alone so I came out here to eat where you could see me."

Father listened to his daughter respectfully but was not finished lecturing, "Maggie how on earth would I be able to see you out here?"

Maggie could not believe what her father had just asked her. For the first time, she spoke to her father in a condescending tone, "Are you serious? There is a window (pointing blatantly behind herself) right here. See? The window is clear. You look out. I look in." Maggie's face was flushed with frustration. She stared up at her father as if waiting for his next argument.

Father just looked at Maggie silently. He had the faintest smirk on his face. The smirk got larger, and larger. He looked as though he was holding back laughter.

Maggie stared at him judgingly, ready to continue the battle of words. Father started to shake. Then he started to chuckle. And then laugh. Maggie lowered her guard. It was quite obvious that he was no longer interested in the back and forth. Maggie was now smiling, trying not to laugh at her crazed father.

"Whaaat?" she implored. "Why are you laughing? What's so funny?".

After a few more bursts of laughter Father composed himself enough to respond, "Maggie (laughing) Maggie, look at the window."

Maggie did so and only saw her reflection. She looked at the sides and up the window to try and see through to the other side. "What happened?" she said, "I could see through it earlier. Maggie tilted her head this way and that to try and get a better angle.

"Maggie, somebody closed the curtain. They must have gotten too hot inside." Father started chuckling again, "How long have you been out here?"

Maggie was relieved that she and her father had reached some kind of common ground. She collected herself, "Oh dad, I have no idea. I woke up from a terrible dream, and I couldn't find you anywhere so I decided to eat and then these people sat down and ohh!!! Oh dad! Something's happened! Something bad. Oh it's not good at all."

Father struggled to keep up with his belligerent daughter, "Whoa, whoa, whoa there. Maggie, it's almost ten in the morning. We've got to get going or we're not going to get to see anything exciting today."

Maggie was not ready yet, "But Dad," she interrupted.

Father would not hear anymore of the matter, "Maggie, you can tell me in the car. We need to get going. To see the geysers." With that father began walking away.

Maggie looked up at her dad in disbelief. "There he goes again," she groaned. She picked up her plate, set it on the busing station next to the french doors, and hurried to catch up with her father.

CHAPTER

17

On their way back to their room, Father wouldn't let Maggie say a word. He was so focused on getting out and into the park that he rushed her into their room, where she managed to grab her backpack, while he filled a small ice chest with food for the day. Then it was back out into the hardwood hallway and down inside of the fascinating, round elevator, into the lobby and outside to the valet kiosk. Maggie had even tried to talk to him while they waited for the car, but his nose was, almost deliberately, buried in a glossy paged, fold-out tour guide that he picked up as he left the lobby.

When their car arrived the valet driver reported to Father, "We noticed you were nearly out of fuel sir, so we had it filled up for you. The tab will be billed to your room."

Father smiled at the driver, "Thank you… (looking down at his name badge) Clarence. Much appreciated." Father patted him on the shoulder and then placed something in his breast pocket. Maggie couldn't help but scowl at the young man who had so easily garnered her father's attention.

"Come on Maggie, let's go!" shot father from the other side of the car. Maggie glared at him grudgingly in response. Father was clueless to Maggie's turmoil. He stood in between the open driver's door and the cab. He paused for a moment, hoping that Maggie would capitulate. She had no motivation to do so. Father raised his eyebrows and leaned his body towards the rear of the vehicle as if signaling for Maggie to take note of something in that direction. She just glared at him in frustration. Father's eyes were even wider, "Peo-Ple Are Wai-Ting!!!" he said deliberately.

Maggie looked to where her father was motioning. Three cars idled patiently behind their car. Maggie could feel her cheeks flush pink with embarrasment.

"Ughh!" she huffed.

Maggie stomped over to the car, opened her door, threw her bulging backpack on the floor board and slammed the door closed. Father hopped in on his side energetically.

"Have a fun day," chimed the valet from the other side of the window. Father smiled and waved back, oblivious to Maggie's exasperation. Maggie just stared ahead, boiling in irritation. If her eyes could shoot lasers, everything in front of the car would be a barren, smoldering wasteland.

"Thanks bud, will do," said Father chiming back to the valet. Then with an eager gesture, he slapped the door closed and sputtered the car away from the lodge.

The car fell quiet. All the familiar sounds of driving came right back as they had over the past few days, but the mood inside the cab was drastically altered. The driver was uncharacteristically jittery and quirky. The passenger was a pressure cooker of volatile gases and compounds, fuming and frothing within, poised to erupt from just the slightest encroachment.

The car rolled gently over smooth black pavement. Lush meadow plants rhythmically whirred by, as if they were on a conveyor belt. Massive trees from the edge of The Black Forest shaded Maggie from, what would be, pleasant morning sunshine. If Maggie had any interest in her surroundings at all, she would have been mesmerized by her incredible surroundings.

Father tapped his fingers on the steering wheel to some tune inside his head. The car slowed at the three way intersection they had used the night prior. A large green rectangular sign, on the opposite side of the road read *"Rim Entrance- 18 miles Right, Yellowsemite River Gorge 45 miles Right, Yellowsemite Lake 2 miles Left, Geyser Fields 20 miles Left, Smokey Range 45 miles Left."*

Father stopped the car only for a moment to read the sign, and then turned the car left, back out onto the main road. He was now ready to end the empty silence within the cab. "You know?" said Father pleasantly, "for only being two miles away, we should be able to see the lake from here."

Maggie said nothing.

Father glanced at Maggie from the corner of his eyes. He wasn't giving up so easily, "They say that thousands of years ago, when the world was warmer, this entire valley was filled with water."

Maggie folded her arms resolutely and only looked forward.

"When the world was warmer," continued Father, "The Great Flat Grey Dirt Desert wasn't a desert at all. It was an expansive valley, just like Yellowsemite."

Maggie was unflinching.

Father mulled his thoughts around for a moment before speaking, "Maybe the lake is on the other side of that row of trees."

The car strolled peacefully across an open meadow towards a wall of charming trees, with snowy white bark. The trees were tall, but not nearly as tall as those in The Black Forest, nor were they pine trees. As the car drew closer, the leaves took shape. They were round and thick like green crackers. They looked like tropical trees, that had fitted to a rugged mountainous lifestyle. Just before they reached the grove of trees, another three way intersection emerged reading *"upper valley 30 miles -Right, North Entrance- 60 miles Right, Geyser Fields- 18 miles Left, Smokey Range- 43 miles Left"*. Father once again paused only long enough to read the sign, and then turned left. The cab was once again awkwardly silent as the monotonous sounds of the road increased in volume.

"Don't you want to know where we're going today?" asked father.

Maggie shifted in her seat slightly and fiddled with her ear. "No, not really," she said quietly.

Father must have mistaken Maggie's "no" for a "yes".

He continued excitedly, "Oh, you're going to love it. First, we're going to the geyser loop. Then, we'll drive to the upper valley in the afternoon and see if there's any bison or elk herds grazing. Last, if we have enough time, we'll go to the fossil beds at the far end of the park."

Maggie heard nothing her father had just said. Her stomach turned with all of the recent alarming events that were occurring around her. "I need to tell you something Dad. Well actually, I'd like to tell you a few things," Maggie said softly.

Father squeezed the steering wheel tightly and clenched his teeth. "Maggie," he stammered. "What? What could possibly be more important than what we're doing now? Your dream? Well what about my dreams? Let me tell you about my dreams. Every night, I see your mother washing down the river. Just drifting away from you and I, without giving a damn about the two us. Every night, I wake up because I know she's alive, but she won't come home. And I try to be the best father I can to you, but it's not good enough and soon you'll be gone too. And where will I be huh? I'll be waiting... is that what your dream is about? Is it something like that?" Father snarled.

Maggie trembled in her seat. For the first time in her life, she was petrified. The pillar of a man, who supported her everyday, was now as lost and as frail as she.

"Is that what it's about?" he repeated amidst choppy breaths.

"No," she whispered.

"What?" he commanded.

"No!" she pleaded louder in defense.

"Then can it Maggie! You're not going to drown, and we are perfectly safe. Can we please just enjoy the time we have left together?" pleaded Father.

Maggie didn't know what to say. She was caught speechless with too many things to talk about. She really did feel that the bear attack was worth discussing. She really did believe that her dreams foreshadowed of things to come. And now she was concerned that her father, apparently, had nightmares every night about her mom, and also believed that Maggie was going to abandon him any day.

Maggie bit her lip, looked down at her feet and said, "Okay Dad."

The car fell back to an awkward silence.

CHAPTER

18

They pulled into a nearly full parking lot. The land around the lot was rocky and coarse, pockmarked, dimpled and mounded. Groves of short, scraggly pine trees, bore barren branches, except for their extremities which supported small pom poms of long needles. Each tree looked equally awkward and malnourished, like a junkyard dog sporting a manicured coat, like that of a french poodle. The trees obscured any view of The Geyser Fields. People walked to and from their vehicles from all directions. Tour buses stacked up in a long row to one side, while their noisy engines puffed out thick, choking, black exhaust. Father slowly circled the lot and found a small space between a pine sapling and a large boulder. Maggie noticed three official park vehicles stationed within the lot and was relieved at their presence.

Maggie and father stepped out silently. Neither had spoken a word since father's meltdown. Both had felt defeated at how things had transpired and empty inside. Maggie still wanted to speak to him.

"Some vacation," she thought sadly. She inhaled deeply and almost choked on the surrounding smells that rushed into her lungs.

"Puahh!" she coughed. "What is that horrible smell?" she said pinching her nose and wafting the air away from her in defense.

"It's the Geyser Fields Maggie," responded Father. He waited for Maggie to respond back, but she was too preoccupied swatting the skunky air away from her. "It's the sulfur. It's the sulfur that you smell. The geysers are created far underground. They emit all kinds of gases, and vapors, and pools. Sulfur happens to be a stinky side effect of mother nature."

Maggie was unchanged in her discomfort.

"Well, anyways, you'll see. Don't worry, you'll get used to the smell," he said flatly. Father smiled, shook his head, and started walking towards a boardwalk that led off into the ragged groove of small poodle pines.

"This way Mags," he said.

Once again, Maggie found herself pulling up the rear. She noticed several signs lining the parking lot, cautioning of such things as *"Unstable ground, stay only on boardwalk"* and *"Poisonous gas can cause severe bodily injury. Never breathe in vapors"* and *"Geyser pools are scalding. Do not enter"* and *"Never leave children unattended. Geysers and children do not mix."*

"Where's the one that says *'watch out for bears'*?" asked Maggie sarcastically.

"What was that Maggie?" asked Father.

Maggie did not expect to be heard. She was not ready for another argument. "Where are you taking us?" she asked.

Father wasn't giving any hints. "Just a little ways through here," he said confidently giving away just the slightest hint of excitment.

Tennis shoes clapped and creaked over sun bleached, and wind weathered, wood. Large nail heads popped above the surface of the walk, and were polished to a smooth and shiny rust, that caused a tripping hazard to any traveler who did not pay adequate attention to their footsteps.

The catwalk straddled the sparsely adorned terrain with each dip and bend like a child's roller coaster route. Scattered, contorted pine trees looked like impressionist sculptures at an outdoor museum. Maggie and her father walked through the procession without speaking. It was admittedly peaceful and pleasant, with the knowledge that the rangers were nearby. Maggie couldn't help but relax a little walking quietly through the miniature forest. She noticed faint white puffs of steam escaping from the ground a ways off in the trees.

"Is that a geyser?" asked Maggie pointing to the vapors.

Father glanced back at Maggie and then towards the direction she pointed. Without breaking stride, he answered, "That's just a vent. We will see the geysers in a little bit."

The pine trees began to scatter and the ground became rockier, like the surface of the moon. The vents became more numerous. Maggie could hear the hiss of escaping vapor as she passed by one that was near the boardwalk. She looked down into the fissure. It was only about the size of a finger, but it was obviously deep. Maggie felt a bit unsettled as she contemplated what would happen if she were to fall into a larger vent.

The trees continued to thin as they walked further. Several tall puffs of steam were visible above the stunted treeline. A large basin began to reveal itself as the trees continued to diminish. Father and Maggie made their way through the last of the trees, to an overlook of the wide open space below them. The setting was as stunning and breathtaking as it was alien.

It was the size a large soccer stadium, shaped like a crater with slopes rounding down to a central point, except for the far end. On that side was a break that looked like a narrow, rocky ravine. Through it ran a small stream of, what had to be, water containing vivid streaks of red, yellow and orange that coursed through its diminutive current. It looked as though someone had stretched out a saltwater taffy and laid it over the ground, like a thin stretch of carpet.

On the slopes of the crater, several large vents billowed out steam from wide, rocky orifices. They looked like uninviting dragon's lairs. Maggie looked at the slope directly below her. Mineral pools idly steamed and trickled water down to the next pool like perfectly formed stair steps, shaped like a peacock's tail on full display. The pools fanned out elaborately and then trickled steaming water down to the next pool, and so on and so forth until the water reached the basin of the crater.

At the basin of the crater was a truly incredible sight. A deep, and somewhat circular pool was stationed in the center. From the edge to middle of the pool were a mixture of brilliant colors. Darkest blue in the deepest area, which aside from what looked like a miniature, fuming, island of a volcano, rising from the depths, was the center. Then the dark blue transitioned to a bright blue, to green as the pool became shallower. And then yellow to orange, until water lapped at the pools edge where a thin line of blood red finished off the color plate.

Maggie stared into the pool to try and understand what she was seeing. The substrate of the pool was solid rock, mineral-like in composition. She had never seen any rock like it. It look hard and rugged, and had contorted appendages, that plumed out from the main body like thunderclouds. The pool was very deep, and although she had no way of telling how deep, the clarity of the water suggested she was looking fifty feet down into its depths, maybe more. She couldn't see the deepest portion though, nothing reflecting light down in its abyssal deep.

Maggie then looked at the small island in the center. It too was made of the same type of rock as what formed around the pool. The little island volcano even had an open, circular vent on top of it. Perhaps, the most interesting thing about the island was that it did not originate from the center of the pool, but instead protruded out from the far side of the pool and then spiraled out towards the center. White clouds of vapor puffed intermittently out of the hole like an old steam engine.

Maggie took a deep breath and admired the entire setting. "How could the land be so lifeless, while the water is so extraordinary?" she thought.

"Unbelievable," she said aloud. For the first time all day, Maggie actually felt good about something. She smiled sincerely at her father who was already smiling down at her. They both looked at each other pleasantly for a brief moment.

"I thought you would like it," said Father at last.

Maggie smiled wide and giggled shyly. She gazed back out over the basin and took in the scene peacefully. She noticed other unique and intriguing features, that she had not seen when she had first took notice of this strange place. She was more relaxed now, more engaged in the moment. A thought crossed her mind, "Perhaps I should let my guard down a little. Maybe I should try to enjoy where I am. After all, isn't that why we're here?"

"Dad?" asked Maggie

"Yes?" replied Father.

"You wanna go down there?" asked Maggie.

"Sure," said Father. "The trail takes us down over here," he gestured loosely with his left arm.

Maggie looked in the direction he was pointing. A well worn, gravel trail gradually arched it's way around the crater downward until it reached the basin. The path sort of spiraled to the bottom and looked very inviting. Maggie could see visitors stationed at various viewpoints, where points of interest must have been. "Let's go!" said Maggie with reinvigorated excitement.

The two stepped towards the gravel grade and began their march to the bottom. As they descended into the bowl it became much quieter. The air became still as there was no breeze to freshen things up. This observation was compounded by the heavy stench of sulfur that stewed within the volcanic cauldron. Maggie gagged as a reflex to the odor.

"Eww Dad, it smells like rotten eggs... bad!!" blurted Maggie.

Father chuckled quietly and then responded, "Yeah, guess it does smell like Grandpa Jack's house."

Grandpa Jack lived just outside of the city on an Emu egg farm. Maggie had visited several times during summer vacations. Once a week, the farm would process the "dud's" into fertilizer. The process was very messy and made the entire farm smell horrible for a few hours. Maggie instantly understood her father's joke and started laughing out loud.

"Bahahaha," she rolled with laughter. As she gasped for air, the stench filled her nostrils and caused her to gag uncontrollably. She heaved involuntarily at the smell, which only made her laugh harder.

Father watched her gesticulations and began laughing wildly as well. He too needed to inhale deeply, which caused him to heave out the foul stench, and in turn, only caused him to laugh harder. Maggie and her dad, laughed and gagged together until they found themselves kneeling on the ground with their hands braced to the gravel in a futile attempt to regain composure. A group of hikers passing by stared at the two in bewilderment. They did not stop, but we're obviously concerned about Maggie and her father, and did not find the stench so amusing.

Eventually, the two regained composure. Their stomachs could resist the urge to purge. They stood up breathing hard, still suffering from the all-encompassing odor, but feeling emotionally refreshed. For Maggie, the laughter was cathartic. She had carried her stress and fear for too long. The laughter had washed it away as though she had bathed under a tropical waterfall. She felt good, despite the nasty smell that besieged her. Maggie looked at her father and smiled wide at him. She was not as resentful towards his standoffishness nor the indelicate behavior that had predominated his character over that last couple of days.

At that moment, Maggie felt a little bit older, and wiser. She still loved him as only a daughter could love a father, but he was no longer the stalwart hero who would forever protect her from the woes of the world. He was flawed and penetrable, just as she, and carried a heavy burden of imperfect life experiences that had the power to summon brash behavior and a selfish defensiveness. Maggie looked deeply into his soft, vulnerable gaze. She respected him for who he was, and was grateful for his company, and grateful to be where she was. She still did not understand the looming threats that squalled within the weather of her mind, and it was now abundantly clear that he would not be able to support her with these ailments. Maggie would have to face them alone.

CHAPTER

19

They reached the bottom of the basin in high spirits. They felt like explorers walking upon a strange new world. The unique aspect of being in a crater is that anything beyond the crater is out of sight, and therefore, easily out of mind. The many unique and intriguing features of the crater were the only things captivating their attention.

There was no plant life to observe, but there was much activity all around. Steam escaped out of cavities in the earth in several places that Maggie had not observed at the viewpoint from above. It gave the impression that beneath the ground was a molten soup, mixing and churning and boiling in a pressure cooker far below.

Thick, gloopy pools of mud popped, and hissed, and fizzed like a witches brew. They spewed and sputtered resembling sounds that might be made in the belly of a giant. Maggie was close enough to the vents to see them clearly. They were dark, narrow crevices that spewed out vapor and heat, as if the heat had ripped open the ground as the only means of escaping. There was something very eerie about being next to them. Even the small ones gave the impression that something powerful and dangerous dwelled inside of them. The rock and soil around the crevices was completely bleached of color, as if the heat had scalded away anything capable of supporting life.

The trail lead them down to the basin next to the small colorful stream. The stream was completely unnatural. The water looked more like paint than water. Thick strands of reds, yellows and oranges flowed the length of its course. Several other visitors were stooped over the stream taking photos and carrying on conversations of bewilderment regarding the colorful flow of water.

"It's from the heat and the minerals interacting with the water," answered Father, as if Maggie had asked a question.

Maggie looked up at father curiously.

"The colors are caused by," he went on, "bacteria and algae living in the water. Each species prefers a different amount of light, temperature and chemistry. That's why this little stream and that big pool are so colorful. Anytime you see a different color that means there is a different form of life that survives there. Don't drink the water though... trust me."

Maggie eyed her father suspiciously, trying to decide whether to believe him or not. She hadn't read about any place in the park called *"Geyser Fields"* and therefore knew nothing about where she was. "Anything else, Professor Dad?" she said chidingly.

"Well yes actually," said Father firing back. "At certain times in the year some of the algae will change their color. It's during what is called an "algal bloom" some of these colors get even more bright. One species in particular glows at night in a bright green color."

Maggie didn't know what to believe. She looked at her dad with her mouth slightly ajar. "Huh..." she said at last.

"Look at that!" shouted someone nearby.

"Get back! Get back!" warned another person farther away.

Maggie and her father looked in the direction of the commotion. The little volcano in the center of the deep colorful pool was spewing out water. At first it surged up a little bit, like a thick fountain, and then receded sharply back down, allowing water to splash onto the surface of the pool. Then it resurged with greater force. Water splashed out of the little volcano several feet straight up into the air with steady, thrusting force. The fountain briefly lost its force and dropped halfway in size for a moment, but just as quickly as it lowered in size, the geyser returned with even greater strength. A plume of water shot out twenty feet in the air. Then thirty, still rising to forty, and then fifty feet skyward. People who were close to the pool had quickly made their way back to where Maggie and her father were. The geyser continued to spout higher and higher.

"Dad, are we safe right now?" asked Maggie obviously concerned.

"Umm," mumbled Father. "Umm, yeah." he answered.

Maggie was not convinced by his weak response. She began stepping farther away from the geyser and closer to the trail to exit the crater. Just in case she needed to evacuate in a hurry. She looked behind her as she stepped cautiously backwards. That's when she noticed the ravine.

She had seen it from the viewpoint, but with all the features of the crater being far more impressive and captivating, she had pretty much forgotten about the ravine. She was very close to it, due to where the trail reached the basin. Its narrow walls were sharply cut and jagged. Maggie could see a couple slits of blue sky escaping from the other end of the ravine, suggesting that it wasn't very far to the otherside. The painted stream flowed right down the middle of it. It looked as if a worn trail traveled beside the stream through the ravine as there was a clean depression of dirt running parallel with it, not to mention a few recent shoe prints leading in that direction.

Maggie looked back at the geyser. It had grown in height so high that it looked as though it had reached the top of the crater. A cool mist of vapor began to sprinkle her face. The geyser must have caught a breeze above the crater causing the spray to reach her and the other onlookers. It was a spectacular sight to behold.

"Does this happen all the time?" asked somebody beside her.

An older gentleman, fully outfitted with expensive hiking gear, answered back, "No, this does not happen all the time. In fact, the last eruption was over seventy five years ago."

The small crowd that had gathered, all responded with "oohs" and "ahhs". Some people were clicking away photos with expensive cameras.

"Are we in danger?" asked Maggie to the older gentleman.

"What's that dear?" asked the old man gazing down at Maggie. He replayed her question in his mind and then responded promptly, "Danger? No, I don't think so... but maybe we should move farther back. Just in case."

Maggie turned back around. There wasn't much space left in the viewing area. It was either step back onto the unofficial trail that ran beside the stream, or start heading back up on the trail they had come in on. Maggie was not in the mood to take any chances. She started stepping back towards the exit trail. That's when something caught her eye.

Maggie stopped in her tracks and looked back at the entrance of the ravine. "I could've sworn I saw something blue right there," she thought. She stared at the colorless ground a few feet from her.

"Was it a bird?" she thought.

Maggie didn't flinch. She was certain she had seen something. Whatever it was was hiding right next to her. If she searched long enough, she could find it. She took a slow step closer to the ravine and the creature was forced to flush out.

It was a bird, about the size of Maggie's hand. It's head, breast, back and tail blended perfectly into the chalky grey terrain of the crater, which was why she couldn't see the bird when it was moving. The underside of its wings however, were an iridescent, sapphire blue. Whenever the bird flew, it revealed its azure underside. It was a dazzling specimen.

"A rock tananger," piped Maggie with exuberance.

Maggie had read a little bit about them when she was researching Yellowsemite. She recalled that the rock tananger was incredibly rare and inhabited thermal areas throughout the park. They were revered by bird enthusiasts as a "lifer" bird.

The bird fluttered up a few feet and then clumsily flopped back to the ground a few feet farther away from Maggie. "Oh no," said Maggie, "It's hurt. Dad, dad, there's an injured bird right there. I think it got hurt by the geyser somehow."

Father was transfixed by the geyser. "Oh no," he replied dismissively. He didn't even look in the direction Maggie was indicating. He was too caught up in the moment to worry about some bird.

Maggie had turned away towards her father, once again losing sight of the tananger. She darted her eyes over the area that the bird had landed, but once again, it had disappeared against the backdrop of shadows and patchy rock. She stepped closer towards the tananger and it lifted up into the air, sputtered like a stalling airplane, and flopped a few feet farther away, inside the ravine.

This time Maggie didn't dare take her eyes off of it. It was perched on a small ledge just above the floor of the ravine. The small feathered creature held one wing out as if it was unable to fold it against its body. The bird stayed motionless like a statue. Maggie held her hands out as if gesturing for the bird to hop into her open palms.

"Dad?" asked Maggie as calmly as she could.

"Yes Maggie?" he answered back.

Neither of the two were really paying attention to the other. One was fixated on the geyser, the other on a wounded animal. Maggie took another step closer to the rock tananger. She didn't realized that below her, right beside her shoe, lay two perfectly camouflaged eggs that the tananger had been incubating. Maggie, and the sizeable crowd next to her, had ventured too close to the bird's nest. Forcing the bird to flush out and distract any threat away from its precious eggs.

"I think we should help this bird. It looks hurt," said Maggie.

Father didn't respond at first. He just gazed in awe at the incredible fountain shooting out in front of him. "Ahh," he said at last. "Okay, just be careful."

And with that, Maggie stepped closer to the bird, her body hunched low to the ground so as to not frighten the bird, hands cupped out in front of her, inviting the creature to her embrace. Maggie stepped steadily closer. The tananger cocked it's head to inspect Maggie's movements, and then clumsily flew a few feet farther into the ravine.

"Come here," said Maggie sweetly, "come here, pretty bird."

The bird again cocked it's head to the side and watched Maggie encroach. Maggie felt a deep connection with the bird. She just knew that the bird would trust her, so long as she didn't scare it away and she would be a hero. She had never caught a bird before but, if she did, there had to be some rehabilitation facility that could take it in and care for it.

"Come here pretty bird," she said soothingly.

The bird hopped back a foot, and then another, and then once more. It now balanced on one foot, the other tucked into its stomach. It's wing outstretched even farther.

Maggie sighed and let out a quiet chuckle in humility. "How silly of me," she thought, "why would this little bird just want to hop into my hands? Even though it's obviously hurt, it still is not going to just jump into my hands. I could only imagine how scared it is, having to hide from all of those people, unable to fly."

"Come here pretty bird, I won't hurt you," said Maggie.

The procession of cat and mouse (or more appropriately bird and girl) repeated itself several times. Maggie had tried every technique she could think of to lure the creature. She tried crawling on her belly with only a raised, outstretched finger forward, pretending to be a perch. The bird only hopped farther away. Her clothes tinged with dust, she stood up and reached into her pocket to pull out a handful of trail mix to entice the bird. Again it hopped farther away from her. All too soon, the two had exited the ravine and were now out in the geyser fields.

If Maggie had been aware of where she was, she might have been a little more cautious. For the geyser fields were a gently sloping field of short grass and glacially polished boulders. Mixed in and amongst the boulders and grass were geysers. Some geysers were quite easily seen as they had miniature volcanoes, just like the one inside the crater. Others were nothing more than small, open holes in the ground, that were nearly covered over by the short grass.

Maggie should have also looked around her to see that she was on a wide, gradually sloping plateau that descended down to the meadows of Yellowsemite Valley a couple miles away. She should have looked in the opposite direction to see that she was at the base of a small, but impressive mountain range. Perhaps most importantly, she should have noticed that she was completely alone and out of earshot from anyone who could help her if she encountered a threat.

Maggie hadn't noticed any of her new surroundings. She didn't even hear the steady sound of rushing and churning water. A nearby river coursed its way steadily through an ancient lava flow that had long since solidified into a deep gorge with sheer, vertical walls of black basalt, only footsteps from where Maggie and the flightless bird now sparred.

Maggie took no notice of anything except for the poor bird. At this point she was nearly frazzled with frustration. She had given up talking sweetly to the bird. "Why won't you let me help you bird?" she scoffed. "Something's going to eat you if you don't let me help you," she pleaded.

The tananger continued to lure Maggie farther and farther away out into the field. It flitted all the way to the dark ledge of the rushing river and then rested. The bird held out its wing, a radiant blue reflected off its underside in the midday light. Maggie stared at the bird, baffled. She felt as though her good nature was being taken advantage of. If she moved closer, would the bird try to fly across the gully? As Maggie weighed the bird's options, she began to take notice of her surroundings.

The powerful river was definitely audible. It was loud enough to drown out normal conversation. The tananger was perched on the rough, black ledge right at the steep drop-off to the water. Maggie couldn't see the water from her position but it sounded as though it would be quite a plummet if the bird were to fall. The water was certainly moving too fast for the bird to survive any attempt at swimming.

"I'd better not press my luck," thought Maggie. "If it tries to fly farther, it will surely fall into that river."

Maggie and the bird stared at each other. Then maggie looked back at the ravine. She was quite a ways from it. She wondered if her father knew where she was. "Did he see which way I went?" she thought.

An uneasiness crept into her stomach. Suddenly, she felt quite vulnerable. She looked back at the bird. It was still there, watching her. Maggie no longer felt compassion for the bird. She instead felt like she was the brunt of a joke. "You don't want my help?" said Maggie in frustration. "Fine! But, you do need to go back in your home."

Maggie stepped back a few feet and then circled around the bird uphill of it. Maggie thought if she came from a different angle, the tananger might try to fly back into the ravine. Maggie had given up on the notion that the bird would come to her willingly. Still, she did not want to leave it stranded out of the security of its habitat.

"Maybe someone else can help me catch it," she thought aloud.

The bird watched as Maggie changed tactics. Maggie sidestepped upstream of the bird until she too was along the ledge of the river. She looked down into the water. "Whoa," she exhaled in alarm.

The drop off of the ledge was significant, with gully walls that were vertical and jagged. The river was not very large, but because of its narrow flow and steep gradient, it was certainly not swimmable.

Maggie shook the fear away from her and refocused her attention to the tauntingly wounded bird. She hunched forward once more and slowly stepped closer to the tananger. With Maggie's first movement towards the creature, it lifted its wings and flew quickly away, back into the ravine and out of sight. Maggie watched the bird fly away, utterly baffled at what had just occurred. If only she had known the bird was only protecting its precious eggs. It had fooled Maggie by pretending to be wounded luring her away from the nest.

"It could fly the entire time?" she yelled aloud.

A growl erupted from a short distance behind her, interrupting her moment of exasperation. She hunched her shoulders forward and tried to slowly sink lower to the ground to become less conspicuous. Maggie quivered in fright. The growl was not from a small animal, nor it did sound like a harmless growl. Maggie was in grave danger. She could feel it.

She panted fiercely as adrenaline filled her arteries and veins. "Run, run run!" her brain screamed at her to move. Her muscles were frozen. "Run you idiot!" screamed her brain. A cold sweat began to form on her brow. Every hair on her body stood on edge. Her hands and fingers became clammy and numb from increased blood flow.

She had to turn around to see what growled at her.

"Maybe it's just a honeybadger," she lied to herself.

"You can do it Maggie, you can turn around," she said aloud, trying to sound encouraging. She had to do it. It sounded close. Could she run back into the ravine? She would never make it to safety if the animal was faster than her.

"I can do this," she said aloud trembling. "Just turn..." she turned around to face her foe. She saw it in plain, unobstructed, sight. "...around," she whimpered.

It was not a honeybadger. It was not a mammoth. It was the one animal she knew not to cross paths with.

"Bear," she whimpered.

CHAPTER

20

She knew in that instant that her life was in grave danger. One thousand thoughts rushed through her mind at the same time; every action that had occurred, that led up to this pivotal moment. Every word of wisdom given to her by her father, Sheriff Caldwell, and the old man Bart. The scripture of adventure written in the accounts of Johnny Muur. She replayed the visions she had experienced in her mind in attempt to conjure a plan of escape from this massive, abominable menace. Maggie's body quivered and trembled. Her breath was short and rapid as she desperately sought out sanctuary. She replayed the conversation she had overheard earlier in the morning at breakfast, the one between the park officials. The conversation that warned of how dangerous the short faced bear could be. And now Maggie had inadvertently put that conversation to the test.

Maggie spun around quickly, on shaky legs, to confront the bear. The beast was still facing her, staring her down, studying Maggie's every movement. The savage creature sulked no more than fifty feet from her. Even at that distance Maggie, could see she was no match for the massive brut.

Maggie eyed the ravine, "Can I make it?" she contemplated. The bear growled, as if sensing Maggie's fool hearted plot to escape. "No way." she thought, "There's no way I'll make it in time." She was futily correct.

The tananger had led her too far away from the security of her father, and other visitors, and most importantly, the park staff. If she fled back towards the crater, and the bear took chase, she would surely be overtaken before she even got into the ravine. She recalled what had happened to the boy who was attacked the evening before. There were no mammoths to come and protect her out on the ledge. She was completely alone in this ordeal. Only she could prolong her young, fragile life.

Maggie looked back at the predator, all the while racing in her mind to hatch an escape plan. The bear stood much taller above the ground on long, strong legs. Even on all fours it towered nearly two feet above Maggie. Piercing dark claws protruded from furry paws large enough, and strong enough, to snap a tree trunk from its base with one angered swipe. The beast lowered its muscular, boxed shaped head. It's mouth was slightly agape. A grim set of flesh ripping incisors and canine teeth shone within its mouth. The bear began stepping swiftly to the side a few paces, and then returned back just as quickly. The bear repeated the process again, and again. All the while, never taking its unremorseful, glowering eyes off of Maggie.

"He's going to charge me," whimpered Maggie. She dared not move, she dared not make a sound. She needed time to evaluate her dire situation. "He can outrun me," calculated Maggie. "There's no way I can get back to the ravine. Do I play dead?"

The bear snarled at Maggie. It was a deep, sinister roar that chilled Maggie's bones. The roar echoed across the open landscape. Maggie's heart pounded like thunder in her rib cage. She heaved with the knowledge that any attempt to avoid being attacked was utterly futile. Tears began to stream down her panic stricken face.

"Please..." she quivered in defeat. "Please don't eat me," she pleaded.

The bear lowered its cold blooded snout to the ground. It exhaled excitedly, sending small puffs of dust up in front of its nostrils. The beast prepared to charge. No plea for mercy would enter the beast's one track mind. Prey would come easy today.

Maggie struggled to stand on the lifeless, black basalt beneath her trembling feet. She was out of time and options. She screamed a last blood curdling plea for mercy, "PLEASEEEEE!!!!!!!!!"

The bear lunged its mass forward and charged viciously towards Maggie. Each massive paw thudded against the hardened ledge of ancient lava flow, soon to be a bear's butchering block.

Maggie turned and ran wildly in the opposite direction in reflex. Her two shaky legs were no match for the raw power of four muscular shanks, solely focused on bringing a swift end to the innocent child. The brute was almost immediately upon her. Maggie strided frantically alongside the rushing river below her. Even over the sounds of swift, churning water, Maggie could hear the beast close in. Maggie eyed the unwelcoming flow of water for an opportunity.

She had but one option. One solitary chance of surviving this terrible ordeal. As the bear lept forward with open jaws, it clenched down on Maggie's backpack and thrust Maggie onto the cold hard basalt. Maggie screamed and clawed to free herself. The bear thrashed into the backpack, spewing its contents in all directions. By some miracle, Maggie was freed from the shoulder harnesses. She wiggled out and away while the bear remained preoccupied with the backpack. Maggie turned towards the river and thrust herself into the inescapable, tumultuous gorge. Her arms splayed out like a gawky, featherless fledgling. Her legs dangled helplessly as she dropped into the frigid, snow-forged waters.

Maggie's body seized as she splashed into the unforgiving realm. The icy fluid pressure that immersed her, squeezed her senses and disoriented her. For a moment she did nothing but sink helplessly to the churning, stony bottom. Then she regained awareness.

"Swim," she bellowed within her mind.

Like a lethargic, rusted factory coming back into full operation, Maggie strained every muscle bound to her skeleton to fight for survival. She kicked her legs and pumped with arms and kicked, and pumped, and kicked, and pumped and at last broke the surface. She had escaped certain death from the bear and had survived the blind leap into the rushing river, but there was no time for celebrating.

She was now swimming for her life to keep her head above the fast flowing current. She looked back up at where she had jumped. Far up, and behind her, on top of the ledge she could see the furry, box like skull and thick neck of the short faced bear watching her. The animal tilted its head sideways, as if confused as to what it should do next. With no more than a brief pause the bear lumbered downstream along the ledge, still in pursuit of Maggie.

Maggie searched the rugged walls for an exit, a perch to cling to or a crevice to slip into. A rope, a ladder, there had to be a way out. She could find no such opportunity. All the while, the river swayed and flowed fiercely, forcing Maggie to paddle with all her might to stay afloat.

Maggie tried to remember her bearings. She had purchased a hiking map of the park and had studied it's trails extensively. Unfortunately, she had not studied the rivers. She had no idea where she was heading. All she knew was that she was trapped in a swift moving river, being chased by a monster.

Maggie had to focus so as not to inhale, and choke, on river water. She swam on her side with the current, moving her arms in a frantic doggy paddle. She tilted her hips to one side and kicked her legs like slicing scissors. All the while she searched for a place to exit or at least rest. The river careened swiftly to the right. The gorge walls were just as narrow and sheer as ever. The rushing water slammed her against the formidable wall of rock.

"Hugh," she flexed as her body impacted the unforgiving corridor. She instantly felt the sting of several cuts that occurred as her body abrasively scraped against the stark palisade. She fought frantically to get back into the middle of the flow. It was the only option she could afford until a break in the current condition presented itself. She looked back up and behind her. The bear trotted beside the river, intractably focused on following Maggie.

"Ugh," groaned Maggie at the knowledge that she was in a perilous plight. She was beginning to lose strength. Gasping for air and struggling to keep a safe bearing, her body was beginning to tire in the cold water.

The water became swifter and more turbulent. She looked downstream to see that she was about to enter a section of large rapids. Water spilled over and around a bottleneck of submerged boulders. With no end to the rapids in sight, she could only see that she was in for terrible a experience.

As she entered the rapids, the river pulled her over large boulders and dropped her into roiling pools of violent undertows. She was sucked down through cracks between rocks the size of cars and pushed over drops that would cringe even the most expert of white water rafters. Maggie scudded through the onslaught like a leaf caught in a tornado. Her body was numb from the cold and powerful blows of being slammed against the boulders. When at the surface, she clawed at the rocks for grip. She desperately tried with all her might to cling to dry surface, but she was too weak. She outstretched her arms over the rounded boulders and pressed firmly to stay in place. She kicked feverishly to push up above the water. Her lungs burned from the exertion, but the river was too strong. Her legs inevitably got caught in the current and sent her farther downstream, positioned helplessly backwards.

Maggie was quickly losing any strength left to fight. She could no longer react to the constant pummeling she was being subjected to. It was as though her senses had become overloaded. Her vision had moments of black out. She didn't know if her eyes were opened or closed, or if she was so far under the water that there was simply no light. There was a loud ringing in her ears that was either from water trapped in her ear canals or because her head had slammed against a rock. She couldn't orient if she was upside down or right side up. All that Maggie knew for sure was that she was going to die if the river didn't pacify.

Maggie slammed hard on her back after being tossed over steep rapids. Her body went limp and her breathing slowed significantly. She was defeated, nearly lifeless and completely at the mercy of the river. The thunderous roar of rapids grew steadily quieter, as if farther away. Maggie floated on her back at the surface. Her eyes and mouth slung open in numb paralysis and her limbs floated outstretched and limp. Her clothes were shredded. One shoe had been ripped off exposing a grey sock with big, yellow polka dots.

The water had calmed significantly. She could breath without fear of filling her lungs with water. The section of river she had entered was straight and deep. The gorge walls were still as formidable as ever, and somehow the bear had been able to track her journey through the rapids. If she had any fight left in her, she could swim to the side of the river and rest along the wall, but she simply couldn't. She could barely turn her neck.

Maggie clung to consciousness with every remaining fiber she had left. She struggled to hold on and prayed. She prayed to God to be beached on a welcoming shoreline, where she could regain her strength. She prayed to any spirit that was listening to spare her. She prayed that her father would find her and come to her rescue. She prayed to survive whatever lay ahead. Maggie's prayers were the only things she had left. The river had taken everything else from her, unremorsefully, without care or concern. The river had squeezed every ounce of life and energy that this strong, young woman possessed. It left her drifting helplessly, mercilessly, to an unavoidably dismal destination.

Maggie had surrendered. She was no longer defensive. The river was once again victorious. It trumpeted its calls of victory throughout the dark halls of its sacred mountain realm. Maggie was nothing more than a humbled prisoner awaiting final judgement.

Maggie drifted at the surface on her back. Her ears still rang sharply. Her vision faded in and out of clarity. She stared up passed the black, oppressive chasm that entombed her, up into a cloudless blue sky. The sun was nowhere to be found, shrouded by raised earth, and far away. There was only infinite blue.

The canyon walls slowly marched by her as she drifted downstream. A seemingly, endless, unchanging panorama of imprisonment. The water was no longer cold because she was too numb to feel it. She only stared up into the infinite of black and blue.

Then something started to change. The black had disappeared from view and for a brief moment, there was only blue. Maggie weakly opened her eyes wider in attempt to better observe the change. The black walls of basalt had stopped and for a brief moment there was only sky.

The water rolled Maggie's body to its side. She saw blue sky, a far away horizon, and an expansive valley full of life below her. She saw a large swaying river shimmering in an afternoon sunlight directly below her. A dark, narrow band of lush trees lined the opposite bank of the river. A thin band of bright, cream colored sand separated the trees from the river. And though there was no sign of humanity, it was a beautiful home. "How is this happening?" thought Maggie. "Am I flying?"

"Am I dead?" she asked.

The river answered. It turned her body further still. She now saw a highway of snowy white water leading straight into the large river below. Maggie's hair began to sway wildly in the wind. She was no longer in the water, she was falling out of it. She fell like a shooting star entering Earth's atmosphere, and crashed into the water far below with the weight of a continent.

She had been given to another, delivered with a powerful might from a plummeting height. Maggie's body was twisted and pulled in all directions. She was spun like a rag in a washing machine, squeezed, stretched, contorted, and broken so that all the remaining oxygen in her lungs was forced out. Thousands of perfectly rounded bubbles clung to her lifeless body as she drifted away in the deep.

Maggie was now a part of the river, forever bound to it. Her heart thumped inside of her torso and pounded on her skeleton, demanding air. Her bashed and beaten muscles lay lifeless within her skin, but beckoned to be reawoken. Only one small portion of her beautiful mind stayed alive as she became buried in the watery grave. It was an ancient portion, a stubborn portion. Civilizations realized and atrocities committed under its all-commanding influence. Residing in all. Reserved only for the most ultimate and terminal moments of life. It spoke to her as it had spoke to countless others in their final moments. It said one word, "Live."

The river flashed before her eyes. It flashed a bright, brilliant green bolt of lightning. The deep water flashed again, and again. Maggie was immersed in it, like she was set inside of an ignited emerald. The water became warm, perfectly warm. What little feeling of numbness that remained was now being reawakened. She was no longer numb and lifeless. She was alive.

She was more than alive. Her body felt every minute current of water, as though it was talking to her. On both sides of her rib cage she felt hundreds of vibrations running up and down, as if two pianists were banging on her like a grand piano, playing divine music. Maggie smiled with pleasure.

No longer struggling to breath, she had plenty of air. She inhaled deeply and exhaled peacefully without pain. Her injuries were gone, or healed, or had never occurred. She felt healthy, awake and rejuvenated. Maggie look around in wonder in the world of green.

The green began to clear and take definition. More colors emerged in field of view. Rocks took form. Small sticks and weathered trunks of trees lodged themselves in between the rocks. Above her, the sky dazzled like a fluid oil painting. She had never seen colors with such depth or brilliance. Maggie had never seen with such clarity nor definition, as if she had died and been reborn as a mermaid.

Maggie's failed attempt to look at herself, made her realized, her neck would not move the way she asked it to. She became startled, fearing that she had been paralyzed during her struggle with the river. She told her body to move as it always had and her body would not.

Maggie started to panic. Her dreamlike state was becoming very real. She was indeed alive and well inside the river. "No human could survive this," she thought.

She jarred her body in every manner possible to try to inspect herself. In her hurried frenzy while twisting side to side, she swore she caught a glimpse of a large, translucent, heart shaped tail. It was iridescent and lightly spotted. Deep straight lines rayed out from its base like a sunrise.

Maggie twisted again to see what was following her. Again, she saw the tail, just as close as it had been before. She swam in a tight circle suspiciously eyeing her rear. The tail never changed its distance, it just swayed rhythmically from side to side. She could faintly make out the body connected to the tail. Radiant green scales reflected sunlight into her eyes. Maggie stopped swimming. The tail immediately stopped swaying. Maggie circled faster. The tail instantly swam into action.

Maggie stopped circling. She floated motionless in the current. She was slowly understanding the truth. The tail was hers. The scales were hers. A realization played through her mind. The story of Johnny and his love for the emerald trout. The dream she had suffered through with him, and the eagle, and being drug into the river. Johnny and the storm as he ran from the wall of water. Her mother being swept away in the current, trying to save the life of another. It all made sense now. She understood her visions. Maggie had become the emerald trout.

"Mother," she yelled out loud. "Where is she?" Maggie swam rampantly in all directions desperately searching for her. She darted about in the water like a green bolt of light. After several moments of searching, there was; however, nothing else in the water with her.

Maggie slowly swam close to the shoreline. A radiant bed of rounded, goldenrod pebbles shimmered in the shallow water. Small waves lapped up onto the pebbled beach. Maggie looked from beneath the surface at the treeline beyond the beach. Even in the ever moving ripples of water, she could discern each leaf and each twig in the canvas of dense forest with perfect clarity. Maggie surveyed the treeline slowly from left to right, looking for anything that might explain what had happened to her.

As she panned through the scene, she was startled to see the round face of a person looking back at her. Maggie receded into deeper water with a swish of her broad tail. She turned around to inspect the person.

It was a woman. A beautiful woman. A woman that shared many of the features that Maggie had as a human.

"Mother!!!" cried Maggie.

There was no doubt it was her mother. She looked as though she was the same woman from pictures taken when Maggie was just a baby. Maggie's mother smiled wide, with excitement. She was laughing and crying with joy. Maggie slowly swam to the surface and pushed her shiny snout through it, into the open air. The air was harsh and heavy. It smelled thick with unnatural odors that were so strong they clouded her vision, like thick, intrusive vapors escaping a freshly chopped onion. The air that had kept Maggie alive as a human was not capable of supporting her as a fish. It was far too powerful, almost poisonous. Maggie finned herself back under the water, never taking her eyes off her mother.

Her mother laughed and cried. Tears of joy streamed down her face. "I'm free!" mouthed Maggie's mother. "I'm free," she cried. Sarah knelt beside the river bank and rubbed away the tears that poured down her beautiful face. She rested her hands on her knees, and looked sincerely at Maggie through eyes that burned with empathy.

Maggie slowly swam in place, staring up in shock at her mother, eyeing her every feature. "Mom," she mouthed hopefully. Sarah was unchanged in her expressions. Maggie stared on, praying that her mother might making the connection. Sarah never budged. Maggie began to fully understand what had taken place.

The two gazed at each other while the world drifted past. Neither moved for hours. They told a silent story to each other, both hoping to prepare the other for what was to come. Both had come to grips with their fates. They stayed motionless while the world turned on end and set the sun over distant lands. The sky faded away and a billion bright stars lit up the eternal blackness of night.

At long last, Maggie broke the spellbound stare and looked up into the night sky. It was more beautiful than ever before. Maggie's mother followed suit and looked up as well. Sarah smiled with a glimmer of wisdom in her eye. She knew what Maggie was witnessing, though it was not as brilliant with her human eyes.

Sarah sighed contently and looked back into the water at Maggie. Maggie looked back at her mother in awe. Sarah looked at Maggie lovingly. She raised her hand to her lips, and gently kissed her palm. She then cupped the kiss in her hand and held it over the water. Maggie watch unblinking and slowly swam to the surface.

Sarah rolled her hand over and placed her palm to the surface of the water. Maggie pressed her trout lips to her mother's palm and kissed her for the first and last time, an act Maggie had dreamt of since the moment they had been separated.

Then Sarah stood up. Small golden flakes of sand peppered her smooth skin as she rose. She stood over Maggie and stared down at her. Sarah looked excited and apprehensive, like a wild horse eyeing a wide open grassland. She looked around at her surroundings and then back at Maggie. At last she spoke to Maggie in a voice that echoed through the water, through her body, "The river gives, and the river takes. Take the river with you." And with that, Maggie's mother turned slowly away, walked across the beach of pebbles, and disappeared into the forest.

The End

THE RIVER GIVES
PART 1 OF: ESCAPE FROM THE RIVER

CHAPTER

1

A TV had been turned on. A commercial was just finishing its sales pitch, "...but you have to hurry. Supplies are limited." The commercial had ended. The next program was beginning. Sitting behind a large oblong desk, a young reporter was centered in the screen reading off of a list of bullet points on paper. The reporter began speaking, "Thank you for joining us. And now for tonight's top headline. Calamite appears to have struck in Yellowsemite National Park after two young hikers have, allegedly, been attacked by a rampant, wild bear. Park officials say seventeen year old Zachery Nielson was critically injured by the bear, two days ago, while hiking alone, just before sundown. He is currently in ICU at Geyserville Hospital. Doctors say his condition is stable, although he remains unconscious. Park officials then began an extensive search for the large bear but were not able to find it before it attacked a second hiker, thirteen year old Margeret Mursen. She and her father were visiting the Park's geyser fields and, at some point, became separated. Margeret's backpack was found near the Roaring River gorge, a dangerous section of water revered by whitewater enthusiasts. As you can see, the backpack was completely destroyed by the bear. Park officials believe the backpack was ripped off of Margeret. Thus far, neither the bear, nor

Margeret have been located. Park authorities are currently looking for both." The reporter stopped talking and stared blankly into the camera. He placed a finger to his ear as if listening to an instruction that was coming in from an earpiece. "Ladies and gentlemen we are now going to give you live coverge of a press release taking place as we speak. I am being informed that Park President Arthur Greyguse is about to release a statement. Please standby while we bring you live coverage of the briefing."

The screen changed from the completely scripted news studio to, a large conference center. A small podium was centered in the screen illuminated by bright flood lights. It was backdropped by an austere fabric wall, framed by the national flag on the right, and the official park flag on the left. Art was just stepping onto the screen. He was speaking earnestly to somebody off camera as he made his way to the podium. His voice became audible as he got within range of the microphone "...that's fine, that's fine. Thank you Jim." and paused for a moment.

Looking out into the audience, Art began his address, "Ladies and gentlemen, thank you for joining us on such short notice. I'm sure many of you are aware of the challenges that are facing this great park. At this very moment, we have one young man who is currently being hospitalized, a young woman who has been missing for nearly thirty six hours, as well as an aggressive predator running loose somewhere in this venerable park. As Park President, it is my responsibility to ensure that we minimize any further harm to visitors as well as respond promptly and diligently to the dire priorities that have been beset upon myself, and our first responders. For that reason, effective immediately, we are temporarily suspending all wilderness permits that are currently active, or will be active until we have captured the animal responsible for these brutal attacks. Any backpackers, or those staying in primitive campsites will be instructed to report to the nearest ranger staion immediately. We have closed all hiking trails to one eighth mile from their start point. Depending on the degree of success our efforts reward, we may be forced to close the entire park to the public within the next twelve to twenty four hours.

Folks, I cannot stress the degree of concern every individual in this park must have at this time. What I am asking from all of you here with us tonight, is that you remain patient as we work to find Maggie, that you trust that our steps to protect the park and the people inside of it are appropriate, and that you support our first responders fully, in finding this unbridled animal that appears to be actively hunting humans. If anyone should come in to contact with a large predator, in or around the park, please report it immediately to the nearest local law enforcement agency.

Now, as you can imagine, we have many tasks to address at this time so I will only be able to answer a few of your questions. If I did not answer your question please send it to: incidentanalysis@yellowsemite.gov and we will try to answer your concerns as quickly as possible. Now, lets move on to questions." Art looked around the room, pointing, "Yes, you in the back."

A barrel-chested reporter with grey hair, wearing a Hawaiian shirt stood up and asked, "Mr. Greyguse, you mentioned (looking down at his notes) an aggressive predator and an unbridled animal as the culprit of the attacks. Do we have any further information about this animal to better describe it?"

Art furrowed his brow and looked sidways at the reporter, suggesting that he did not want to answer the question. He paused briefly to think, and then answered, "Based on evidence left at both incidents, we are search-ing for something very large and powerful..." Art looked down at the ground pensively. Beads of sweat began to show on his heavy, furrowed brow in the bright artificial light. He ran his fingers across his scalp searching to find the right response, continuing, "The animal is, most likely, a very large grizzly bear weighing about two thousand pounds."

A subdued, but concerned uproar arose from various parts of the audi-ence. Art looked for another person to call on. "Yes miss, there on the side. Yes, go ahead."

The woman stood up. She pinned her shoulders back broadly and held a stiff posture. "Sir, bear attacks, as unfortunate as they are, are a somewhat expected occurrance here at the park. Why do you feel it necessary to enforce such strict measures for something that park visitors are already aware of, if not prepared for?" She sat back down.

Art took a sip from a cup of water that had been stashed within the podium. Again, he looked away pensively to find an appropriate response. He took a large swig of water and then spoke, "Because of the severity of the injuries sustained by mister Nielson... and the potential size and power that this animal appears to display. Yes, it is true. As unfortunate as the truth may be, park visitors, and even staff come into contact with wildlife and injuries can occur to all parties. In this circum-stance, we need to be certain that we are taking every step necessary to resecure this park, and mitigate this threat. Thank you. Last question, yes ma'm, you in the front here."

The woman remained seated. Only a glowing head of curly hair could be seen from the angle of the camera. "Yes, thank you Art, as a resident of the Greater Yellosemite Ecosystem, what concerns should we have about the potential for this grizzly to wander into one of our backyards?"

Art looked at the woman sincerely, "Thanks Judy, im glad you asked that question. My cause for warning also echoes out into the areas surround-ing the park. At this point, we are dealing with a large bear that is untagged, prefers flatland, and can run very fast. Again, I must urge everyone to use extreme caution until our first responders can neutralize this threat, by any means necessary. Now, I thank you all for coming. No more questions." Several voices of reporters shouting questions could be heard as Art walked out of view on the TV screen. The original news reporter came back on screen.

"Well there you have it. Park President Greyguse issuing dire measures and a stiff warning to those in and around the Yellosemite area. Now in other news, lets take a look at the weekend forecast..." the TV turned off.

CHAPTER

2

Two black, glistening eyes peered out from the shade of the undergrowth. The eyes looked forward, then to the left, and then to the right. The eyes looked down at the tranquil pool of a cold mountain stream and paused. A long, slender, wizened tongue lapped against parched, rubbery lips in the darkness. Ever so slowly, four paws stepped forward into dappled afternoon sunlight, onto wet, brown, silty sand. The paws were small, and dainty, but powerful, supporting strong, stilt-like legs. The paws sported clipped fur of charcoal black. The legs bore a longer, mangy coat of cinnamon.

The eyes remained hidden in the shadows. They quickly swayed and bobbed in all directions to ensure the coast was clear. At last, the animal stepped out onto the steep creek bank. A maned wolf, a solitary hunter of high elevation grasslands. Not a wolf, nor a fox, nor a dog, but something in between. If a giraffe and a red fox had a child together, a maned wolf was the outcome. It panted ravenously at the clear, cool water.

Again it stepped closer to the water's edge. It was a beautiful specimen. A long mane of cinnamon fur covered most of its body. A black patch on the shoulders resembled a small cape. Lean and muscular standing high above the ground, its stature and gait resembled that of a ballerina. If it so desired, it could stand stately on two legs and leap high into the air, performing a perfectly balanced ballonné. Its light, tall frame made it easy to understand that this predator was built for pouncing on fleeing prey in high grass. Its long snout housed a full set of white canine incisors. Its ears were cupped and pointed, standing upright equidistantly with its snout.

The wolf decided it was safely alone and stepped to the edge of the water. It folded its front legs, lowered them down to the ground and began to drink thirstily. With each drink from its tongue, small circular waves of motion spread out and slowly covered the calm water, while something stirred beneath the water.

The wolf stopped drinking, stood back in a lunge position and peered into the depths of the pool. Its ears pinned forward instinctively. Nothing stirred below the surface. The rings of water had expanded out far across the pool and disappeared, returning the surface of the stream to a mirror like state. The wolf stood motionless as a lush canopy of tall birch trees swayed gently in the breeze above it. A whip-poor-will sounded far ahead upstream, and bubbles of gurgling water drifted peacefully downstream. The wolf cocked its head sideways indicating that it had seen something noteworthy. Its eyes lasered through the water and stayed fixed on one point of interest.

A green flash of light lit up the pool. The wolf jumped six feet into the air and disappeared back into the lush vegetation. It had kicked so hard running away that small clods of dark silt were flung out into the pool. The clods disintegrated and covered the surface with a speckled film of grit. The sound of hurried steps could be heard as the wolf broke away recklessly through the underbrush.

After a moment, the streamside returned to serenity. The wolf's retreat was no longer audible. The sound of gurgling water, songbirds, and insects filled the air with peace. The film of dirt slowly cleared as it was washed downstream. A large and beautiful trout cautiously swam out of the shadows.

The trout had come from a far away land, and seen many unbelievable things. It could read (if it had a book) and could write (if it had hands).

Truth be told, the trout was far more accustomed to being a human than being a trout, but it was learning. Learning to survive in an alien world. Forced to survive out of necessity. Bound to an underwater way of life.

Two months had past since Maggie, the girl, had leapt into the frigid, rushing waters of the Roaring River in order to spare herself from being eaten by a ravenous bear. She had been nearly bludgeoned to death in the river gorge that swept her downstream and over the falls that poured her into the Flowy River. Lifeless and at the mercy of the river, she was transformed into a spirit of the river and became bound to an underwater realm. In compensation the river released Maggie's mother upon its pebbled banks.

As a trout, Maggie had spent countless days trying to understand what had happened to her and the meaning of the events. For the first two weeks as a trout, Maggie remained at the base of the falls waiting for her mother to return. Waiting for her father to find her, or a search party to come along. No humans ever discovered Maggie's hold. Lofty puffs of summer clouds ambled overhead as tradewinds blew them to new lands. Swallows zipped and fluttered over the current of the river, gulping water. Maggie watched the birds land on the river bank, where they would then mix dirt from the bank with the water stored in the their crops. They would swallow and then mix and then spit the mixture, and then repeat. Once the composition was correct, the swallows would scoop up the concoction back into their gizzard, fly up to the cliff walls next to the waterfall and use the mud to build nests. The world was not concerned with Maggie's plight. She was on her own, completely alone.

She had seen the helicopters summoned to track down the short faced bear. In the first week, they flew over her daily. Maggie jumped out of the surface to try to get their attention. She splashed and thrashed and did every mannerism she could think of to alert the crew, but the helicopter never took notice. At one point she was so desperate, that she swam out of the water and onto the pebbled bank where she had been reunited with her mother. Her body pulsed vibrantly as her limbless body flapped on the shore. Her senses were overloaded as the hot, sun scorched, pebbles burned her skin. Her eyes and airways stung in the open air as though she had chopped into an especially potent onion. Maggie nearly suffocated on that riverbank trying to be rescued. It took every ounce of ability she possessed to return to the water. To make matters worse, no helicopter ever turned around.

Maggie refused to eat. Each day that she waited to be rescued she gradually lost strength. Her thick muscular body began to deteriorate. Her abdomen gradually sucked in. The electric green markings that shot across her body began to dim. Her iridescent skin began to lose its luster. She became sad and weary. The image of her mother's face played on repeat with her fish brain. "Did she know it was me?" she thought. "I know it was her, but why would she come back for me if, to her, I was just some unlucky soul who got stuck in this body? And where is my dad? I swear that man couldn't find north, even if he had a compass to guide him." Maggie remained in the churning water beneath the fall asking a thousand unexplainable questions, all the while losing precious energy.

On the third week, Maggie was beginning to wither away. She had trouble floating upright. Her deflated abdomen pressed against her swim bladder causing her body to go belly up, a dire scenario for a fish to be in. At last, her need to survive overpowered her need to be reunited with her family. "I must eat something,' she thought, 'What am I supposed to eat?"

She had seen leaves and other plant life drift past her in the water column. As a human she had eaten similar things to survive, so Maggie took an apprehensive bite of a drifting leaf.

"Bleh," her trout mouth gagged involuntarily and spit out the leaf promptly. Her stomach heaved with discomfort as though she had nearly poisoned herself. A sensation similar to a human drinking gasoline.

"Maybe I can't eat leaves," she thought, "But what about moss? I could eat moss. Moss is just like… a salad without dressing. I could eat that." Maggie swam over to a nearby clump and took a bite.

"Puh!" Again her famished body heaved out the inedible object with the same fervor as she had rejected the leaf. "Ugh!!" thrashed Maggie. "What am I supposed to eat?" she thought, "It's not like I have a kitchen to just make myself a sandwich." Maggie stopped swimming. Her famished, finned body went limp. She began to drift, like a wayward leaf, downstream, away from the waterfall.

A defeated emerald trout considered the possibility of starving to death. Then something bumped its snout. Maggie was snapped back into the present moment. She focused on the object that had collided with her. "It's a bug!" she thought.

The small creature had a wide, hard body with rigid, serrated sides. Two hind legs kicked out like oars on a canoe. The bug's small body swam in a zigzag direction upwards to the surface of the river. Maggie watched in perplexity as the determined bug broke through the surface like a breaching submarine. Then the insect floated motionless, drifting in the current.

Maggie inquisitively followed the animal closely. As she ascended, the bug began to fidget and writhe. The hardened outer shell separated from the fleshy body within. Maggie's eyes widened in shock. The bug began to split open along its back, as if someone had unzipped the suit it was wearing. Two large moth-like wings protruded out of the open shell and began to quiver and flutter. Within seconds the wings unfolded wider and strengthened. The bug fluttered its brand new wings harder, and flew off into a bush near the river's bank.

"What did I just witness?" gawked Maggie. She followed the lifeless, translucent shell that had been left behind, from the insect's transformation. A water bug had literally transformed into a flying bug in a matter of seconds. Never had she seen or known of such a life cycle.

"I wonder if I can eat that thing?" considered Maggie. Her stomach rolled in empty discomfort. She swam slowly up to the alien exoskeleton. She bumped it with her nose. The hardened skin didn't even budge. "Here goes nothing," thought Maggie. She opened her lower jaw exposing a row of small piercing teeth. Her iridescent gill plates flexed forward. Dark red, feathery gills flashed of a vulnerability that she was better off not knowing about.

Maggie closed her mouth on the small snack and swallowed it whole. "Interesting," she thought, as she crunched on the crispy keratin. "I thought it would have more flavor." She decided to try living as a trout.

In the days that followed, Maggie slowly became accustomed to an aqueous lifestyle. She was always moving, whether she intended to or not. Gravity works differently underwater.

CPSIA information can be obtained
at www.ICGtesting.com
Printed in the USA
FSOW01n1602061217
42117FS